"Thank you, Luke. You rescued me today in more ways than one."

For several seconds Luke's thoughts scattered at the sensation Mary's hand created in his. Soft. Her hand felt so soft and delicately feminine. So...

Misleading.

That was the only term Luke would allow himself to describe his intense reaction to her touch.

As Mary climbed into her truck and drove off with a smile and a wave, Luke couldn't help wondering what he was walking into and how it might be connected to his wife's murder. Mary's truck's punctured tire had his gut shrieking warnings that something wasn't right. Whether Mary was an impostor or not, Luke was afraid for her and her daughter.

This Mary Calder, whoever she was, had an enemy.

Dear Harlequin Intrigue Reader,

What's bigger than Texas…? Montana! This month, Harlequin Intrigue takes you deep undercover to the offices of MONTANA CONFIDENTIAL. You loved the series when it first premiered in the Lone Star State, so we've created a brand-new set of sexy cowboy agents for you farther north in Big Sky country. Patricia Rosemoor gets things started in *Someone To Protect Her.* Three more installments follow—and I can assure you, you won't want to miss one!

Amanda Stevens concludes her dramatic EDEN'S CHILDREN miniseries with *The Forgiven.* All comes full circle in this redemptive story that reunites mother and child.

What would you do if your "wife" came back from the dead? Look for *In His Wife's Name* for the answer. In a very compelling scenario, Joyce Sullivan explores the consequences of a hidden identity and a desperate search for the truth.

Rounding out the month is the companion story to Harper Allen's miniseries THE AVENGERS. *Sullivan's Last Stand,* like its counterpart *Guarding Jane Doe,* is a deeply emotional story about a soldier of fortune and his dedication to duty. Be sure to pick up both titles by this exceptional new author.

Cowboys, cops—action, drama…it's just another month of terrific romantic suspense from Harlequin Intrigue.

Happy reading!

Sincerely,

Denise O'Sullivan
Associate Senior Editor
Harlequin Intrigue

P.S. Be sure to watch for the next title in Rebecca York's 43 LIGHT STREET trilogy, MINE TO KEEP, available in October.

In His Wife's Name

Joyce Sullivan

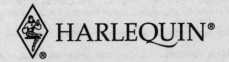

TORONTO • NEW YORK • LONDON
AMSTERDAM • PARIS • SYDNEY • HAMBURG
STOCKHOLM • ATHENS • TOKYO • MILAN • MADRID
PRAGUE • WARSAW • BUDAPEST • AUCKLAND

ISBN 0-373-22631-4

IN HIS WIFE'S NAME

Copyright © 2001 by Joyce David

This edition published by arrangement with Harlequin Books S.A.

Visit us at www.eHarlequin.com

Printed in U.S.A.

ABOUT THE AUTHOR

Joyce Sullivan credits her lawyer mother with instilling in her a love of reading and writing—and a fascination for solving mysteries. She has a bachelor's degree in criminal justice and worked several years as a private investigator before turning her hand to writing romantic suspense. A transplanted American, Joyce makes her home in Aylmer, Quebec, with her handsome French-Canadian husband and two case-book-toting kid detectives.

Books by Joyce Sullivan

HARLEQUIN INTRIGUE
352—THE NIGHT BEFORE CHRISTMAS
436—THIS LITTLE BABY
516—TO LANEY, WITH LOVE
546—THE BABY SECRET
571—URGENT VOWS
631—IN HIS WIFE'S NAME

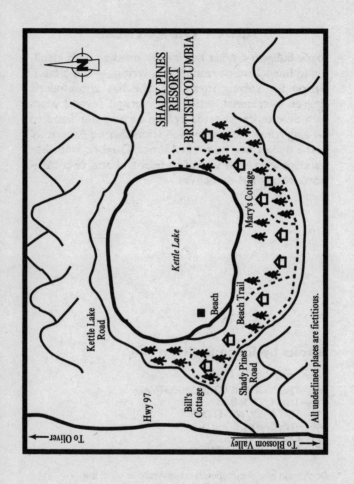

SHADY PINES
RESORT
BRITISH COLUMBIA

Kettle Lake

Mary's Cottage

Beach Trail

Beach

Bill's Cottage

Kettle Lake Road

Hwy 97

Shady Pines Road

To Oliver

To Blossom Valley

All underlined places are fictitious.

CAST OF CHARACTERS

Mary Calder—What really happened the night this beautiful public relations consultant was murdered?

Luke Calder—He was determined to discover who had killed his wife.

Shannon Mulligan—Mary Calder's name gave her a new identity and an escape from her past.

Rob Barrie—He wouldn't rest until he and Shannon were man and wife...again.

Dylan White—What would this teen do to protect his mother's income?

Glorie—The burglary in her gift shop was most puzzling.

Bill Oakes—What could the resort caretaker tell Luke about the woman who called herself Mary Calder?

To Mom and Dad,
My first heroine and hero, who taught me the meaning
of family and commitment and unfailing support.

Acknowledgments

My sincere thanks to criminologist T. Lorraine Vassalo
and family lawyer Marci Lin Melvin, B.A., LL.B.,
for patiently answering my questions about the
Canadian legal system. And to fraud detective
Paul Heagle, Ottawa-Carleton Regional Police Services
(retired), for explaining how the men and women in blue
get the job done. Without you, this story would never
have been more than an idea on a piece of paper.

Thanks also to the following for helping me get the
details right: Jackie Oakley, Ottawa-Carleton Regional
Police Services; Dr. Stephen W. Maclean; Nina Fast, R.N.;
Deborah Sarty; Pat and Linda Poitevin;
and Kay Gregory. Any mistakes are my own.

Last but not least, a heartfelt hug to Judy McAnerin
for her exceptional plot analysis skills!

Prologue

Mary was unmindful of the car tailing hers; its looming headlights in her rearview mirror were insignificant and blurred by the darkness of the night and the sleet lashing her windows. At least her meeting with her client at the country club had gone well, and he'd been open to her suggestions to smooth over his furniture company's image in the media after a consumer's report on the evening news had targeted it for its sales tactics. She didn't know why public-relations crises were like fevers in sick children, which reached a flashpoint in the middle of the night.

Mary smiled, thinking about children. Babies in particular. And making a baby with Luke. Her toes had turned to ice cubes in her black leather pumps. What she needed was a hot bath, candlelight and Luke's long lean body sharing the tub with her.

Mary stopped her sports car for a red light at a dark intersection, her mind drifting to fantasy. Too bad Luke was on duty tonight.

Without warning her door was jerked open. A hand brutally gripped her arm and attempted to pull her from the car.

Mary fought back instinctively. Honked the horn. Screamed at her attacker. In her peripheral vision, she saw a dark-clothed figure dart in front of the headlights—a woman?

Something struck Mary. Hard. Her left arm exploded with pain. Her attacker reached across her body and released her seat belt. As he dragged her free of the car, Mary saw her attacker's face…looked straight into his eyes. Shock came in a frigid thrust she felt to the depths of her soul. In that brief all-knowing instant, Mary knew she wouldn't survive the night.

Chapter One

Sixteen months later

The shrill of the phone literally caught Luke Calder with his pants down. After putting in a ten-hour night shift on the streets in a patrol car, all he wanted was some shut-eye. With a tired sigh, he kicked his jeans toward the laundry pile on the closet floor and reached for the phone beside his bed. "Calder here."

"Constable Calder, this is Alex Hudson from the credit bureau. You asked us to flag your wife Mary's file and notify you of any activity."

Luke's fingers stiffened on the telephone receiver, as his body tensed against the sudden eruption of emotion in the pit of his stomach. The barren sand-colored walls of his bedroom shifted around him as if on motorized tracks. More than a year had passed since Mary's murder, and Ottawa-Carleton's finest detectives and forensic experts—fellow officers Luke had faith in, would trust with his life—hadn't been able to come up with a lead in her murder. The investigation was in limbo—just like Luke's life—delegated to a stack of cold files on a major-crime detective's desk.

He closed his eyes to block out the spinning walls and dredged deep inside himself for the professional control that had been drilled into him at the police academy. *A lead. Oh, God, please let this be a lead,* he prayed. "Has there been some activity?" he bit out.

"Yes," Hudson acknowledged, his husky voice tinged with compassion. "A business-loan application to a bank in British Columbia. A branch in Blossom Valley. It probably would have gone unnoticed if you hadn't flagged your wife's file."

Luke sucked in his breath as his brain computed the significance of the information through an insulating layer of shock. When he'd made the request of the credit bureau after Mary's purse was stolen during the assault and attempted carjacking, he'd been more worried about the perpetrator running up Mary's credit cards to her limit, not fraudulent bank loans. But still, there could be a connection, however remote. "Did the applicant give a current address?"

"Only a box-office address in Blossom Valley. Have you got a pen?"

"Just a sec." Luke reached for his black duty bag, which he'd tossed on the bed a few minutes ago. After a moment's fumbling with the zipper, he produced a pen from a side pocket, then grabbed for a notepad, a woodworking magazine resting on the oak bedside table he'd made Mary as a first-anniversary gift. "What have you got?"

Hudson read off the address.

Luke jotted it down, forcing his hand to form each letter. His fingers had turned to rubber. "Thanks, I'll take it from here." His knees gave out as he hung up the phone. Luke sank onto the bed, his heartbeat spiking and his thighs shuddering as if he'd just chased down a perp. Nausea swirled in his stomach as he pressed his forehead to his bent knees, but there was no way to avoid the anguished images that twisted him inside out—images of Mary dying in fear…in pain…without a cop in sight to save her. Much less her own husband.

He'd been on duty that night. Mary had died before she'd reached the hospital. He hadn't even had the chance to tell her that he loved her one last time. Why hadn't she just let her assailant have the damn car?

A sob caught in his chest, building until the pain of it vibrated through his body and throbbed in his brain. His fingers clutched the magazine like a lifeline to sanity. Would this address lead him to Mary's killer?

THERE WAS SAFETY living in a small town. Shannon Mulligan could look out the window of Glorie's Gifts Galore—one of the many shops in British Columbia's Okanagan Valley where her handmade crafts were sold—and easily scan the six-block length of Blossom Valley. She knew the proprietor of every store in the Western-style business district by name and every face that belonged here. Strangers stuck out like palm trees in a desert and made her hackles rise until she assured herself that the stranger couldn't possibly be her ex-husband.

Surely the fact that Rob hadn't found her in sixteen months meant he likely never would. She and Samantha were safe.

As if knowing she was the object of her mother's

thoughts, nine-month-old Samantha gurgled and cooed with delight as her plump sweet fingers latched on to a bright red apple appliquéd to the green gingham skirt covering a nearby display table. A basket filled with vegetable- and fruit-shaped napkin rings nearly slid off the table as Samantha tugged on the tablecloth. Shannon expertly grabbed the basket to prevent it from crashing to the floor, then worked the gingham cloth from her daughter's grasp.

"Oh, you silly girl!" she admonished gently. "The apple is so pretty and colorful, isn't it?"

Samantha beamed up at Shannon from her stroller, her cap of silky dark hair mussed and her dark eyes glinting with smoky-gray and mottled-brown flecks of mischief. Eyes so like Rob's, Shannon's ex-husband, that they irrefutably confirmed the truth of Samantha's sordid conception. Shannon prayed daily that her baby hadn't also inherited her father's tendency to fly into rages at the slightest provocation.

So far, Samantha's temperament had been as meek as a lamb's. Despite the terror and uncertainty that had hounded Shannon during the days and nights of her pregnancy, she loved her daughter more than life itself. Because of Samantha, Shannon had found a courage inside herself she hadn't known she possessed. She'd taken risks, impossible risks, but they'd all been worth it. Rob would never be able to lay a hand on her again.

Her eyes stung with tears as she bent to kiss her daughter's brow. Samantha deserved a safe and happy childhood. That was all that mattered.

"Not to worry, Mary," Glorie assured Shannon,

bustling up beside them and breaking Shannon's train of thought. "I should have offered to get the door for you, but I just couldn't take my eyes off that batch of birdhouses you just brought in. I promised to put one aside for a customer."

Shannon could see by the genuine softening of Glorie's careworn face that the gift-shop proprietor truly didn't mind Samantha's inquisitive fingers. Glorie's heart was as generously proportioned as the body that housed it, and sometimes Shannon felt certain the residents of Blossom Valley would forgive her for assuming another woman's identity. It wasn't as if Shannon was doing Mary Calder any harm. She was just borrowing her name and her likeness.

Shannon eased Samantha's stroller out of the aisle as Glorie pulled the door open. "Now don't forget, Mary, you promised you'd drop off a dozen welcome signs and at least three letter boxes before the long weekend. I can't keep them in stock. Your Garden Patch collection is just taking off."

"And I couldn't be happier," Shannon replied with a sigh of contentment, feeling grateful that her new career fulfilled both her creative and her financial needs. She was making plans to buy additional tools and to hire someone with woodworking experience to cut the wooden pieces for her crafts so she could concentrate on the finishing and painting. Unfortunately the business loan she'd applied for at the bank to allow her to move her business out of the lakeside cottage she rented and into a larger place of her own had been denied, but Shannon was sure that had more to do with her short residency and lack of employment history.

Her income was steadily improving. She just had to prove to the bank she was a good risk.

Promising Glorie she'd be back in a few days with her order, Shannon pushed Samantha's stroller out onto the sidewalk. July sunshine bathed her face and bare arms with ovenlike warmth. The newspaper office was two doors down. She entered and made arrangements for her Help Wanted ad for a woodworker to be inserted in the upcoming *Weekly Gazette*. Now all she had to do was make a quick trip to the lumberyard for supplies, then head home to put Samantha down for her afternoon nap. Shannon did all her cutting while her daughter napped, looked after business details and sketched designs during the mornings, then painted at night after Samantha was in bed.

Her step quickened and she felt like singing with happiness as she pushed Samantha's stroller toward the beat-up green pickup truck she'd embellished with decorative artwork advertising her Garden Patch collection. A billboard on wheels.

She'd fastened Samantha into her car seat and was climbing behind the steering wheel when she noticed the toy rattle tucked beneath the windshield wiper. What on earth?

Shannon climbed out of the truck and removed the pastel-pink bear-shaped rattle. She'd never seen it before in her life. It looked brand-new. Had someone found it on the sidewalk and assumed it belonged to her because they'd seen a car seat in the truck?

Shannon glanced up and down the street. There wasn't a person in sight. So why, then, did she feel vaguely uneasy as she climbed back into the truck?

FROM A DISTANCE the woman leaving the newspaper office bore a striking resemblance to Mary—bare shoulders tanned a golden brown, the sun glinting off flaxen hair carelessly sweeping sculpted cheekbones. The exuberant bounce in her step as she pushed the stroller down the sidewalk seemed so bitingly familiar that Luke's heart twisted with an impossible wish that the past sixteen months of his life had been some cruel hoax. But reason told him that Mary's death was real. He'd identified her battered body.

Still, from the moment he'd spotted her double leaving the cottage at nine-fifteen this morning, the back of her truck loaded with boxes, this woman with the baby—whoever she was—affected him like a channel surfer punching the remote control of his emotions. Luke experienced flashes of white-hot rage, stomach-knotting confusion and sharp pangs of unsettled longing as he tracked her movements to three different gift shops in the area. Was it mere coincidence that she shared his wife's name and likeness? Had the credit bureau made a bureaucratic error? Or was something else going on? How many Mary Tatiana Calders with the same birth date could there be in one country?

He was going to call Ottawa on his cell phone and have her license plate run when he got back to the motel. He dropped a tip on the coffee-shop table where he'd sat the past half hour conducting his surveillance and hustled outside to his rental car. The woman in faded jeans and a white sleeveless cotton blouse was just starting the engine of a brightly painted pickup that made following her child's play.

Before he'd been granted emergency leave and

hopped the first flight he could to Penticton, the Okanagan city nearest Blossom Valley with an airport,
Luke had called Detective Sergeant Zach Vaughn, the
lead investigator in Mary's murder, to inform him
what was up. Vaughn had tried to dissuade him from
checking out the lead. Department policy discouraged
officers from investigating cases involving family
members. But since they both knew Luke had a right
as a citizen to investigate his own case, Vaughn had
agreed, with certain conditions. Luke was an informant
traveling on his own time, with his own funds—
though he still had a badge that could grant him certain
privileges with the local police. Luke was to keep in
constant touch with Vaughn. The minute Luke found
any evidence linking this woman to Mary Calder's
murder Vaughn would call in the local police to take
over the investigation.

After Luke had agreed to the conditions, Vaughn
had checked the police computer and found out the
woman had a British Columbia driver's license, which
gave Luke the street address the credit bureau hadn't
been able to provide.

Luke eased into the traffic behind a dusty black
coupe with a dented right fender. This Mary Tatiana
Calder didn't go far, just to the hardware store on the
west end of town. Luke pulled into the parking lot a
good two minutes behind her, then sauntered into the
store while she was wrestling the stroller out of the
bed of the truck.

He planted himself near the book display just inside
the entrance, fanned open the pages of a how-to book
on wiring and waited. Suddenly the automatic doors

swung inward and Luke heard the woman's muted voice talking to the infant. But he lost track of the words as his gaze took in the baby girl propped up in the stroller and wearing a pink sundress that reminded Luke of cotton candy and all things feminine. Her full round cheeks, dark silken hair and wide gooey smile caught him like an arrow to the heart.

Once upon a time he and Mary had dreamed about having children. Planned for it. They'd even had names picked out. Nothing too fanciful like Tatiana, which Mary had hated as a child. Simple solid names like Ryan and Laura.

Pain Luke thought he'd banished clawed at his throat as his gaze trailed upward toward the baby's mother. The shape of her oval face enhanced her startling resemblance to Mary, but only superficially. Even as his body registered the woman's beauty, his brain logically picked out subtle differences—the nose that was longer and delicately pointed, the smattering of freckles across her cheeks, the smile that was wider. Eyes that were more hazel than blue. And from his vantage point he could see the telltale traces of natural-brown roots in her dyed blond hair.

He ducked his head behind the pages of the wiring book as the woman's gaze swiveled past him. Instead of moving directly into the maze of plumbing and electrical-parts aisles, she turned toward the customer-service desk. Luke watched as she stopped in front of a bulletin board mounted on the wall near the desk and removed from her denim purse a piece of paper, which she posted on the board.

She seemed to be scanning the board with interest,

then with a sigh, turned and headed right past him into
the store, close enough for him to become acquainted
with the exotic scent of her perfume, which made him
think of hot summer nights and jasmine. Luke hid his
face behind the book until he was certain she'd passed,
then casually moved over to the bulletin board.

The Help Wanted notice she'd posted gave him all
the excuse he needed to make the woman's acquaintance.

AWARE OF THE TIME, Shannon hurriedly buckled her
daughter into her car seat as the yard clerk loaded her
lumber order into the back of her truck. It had taken
longer than she'd anticipated to select and purchase
the knot-free planks she needed; now she was worried
Samantha might fall asleep before they got home. Taking a nap in the car, even a short nap, usually screwed
up her daughter's sleeping schedule, and Shannon
needed to start cutting the pieces for the signs and the
letter boxes today if she was going to fill Glorie's order as promised.

Shannon climbed into the cab, slamming the door
behind her. The engine ground for a second, then sput-
tered into life. She breathed a sigh of relief and popped
a children's cassette into the tape player, hoping a
sing-along would keep her daughter awake and enter-
tained for the next twenty minutes.

Cheerfully warbling a silly ditty about lost little
ducks, Shannon turned onto the highway. Blossom
Valley, located in close proximity to Canada's arid
desert region of Osoyoos, was framed by rugged hills
covered with sagebrush and antelope-bush and the oc-

casional stand of ponderosa pine and cottonwood. Orchards of ripening peach, apricot, apple and cherry trees lined the highway, and vineyards crept up the hills, irrigated by the many crystal-blue lakes that abounded in the Okanagan.

Shannon had picked this area because her aunt Jayne, who lived in Halifax and knew the bleak cold rain of the Maritimes, had toured the region with a friend several years ago and had come home raving about the dry climate.

A few minutes outside of town, the highway climbed, winding between a lake and a ridge of mountains. The curves were sharper. Shannon felt an insistent tug on the steering wheel as it seemed to resist her efforts to stay in her lane. What was going on? With fear mounting that they might plunge off the road, she reduced her speed and gripped the wheel tightly.

The truck continued to lean to the right, and it took Shannon a full minute before she realized she probably had a flat tire. There was no shoulder here where she could safely pull over, but she knew there was a lookout over the lake not far ahead. Knuckles white with fear, Shannon slowly negotiated the curves, feeling as if she was trying to coax a recalcitrant bull into submission. By the time she pulled safely into the lookout, her heart was pounding and her face was damp with perspiration.

Now what? She didn't belong to an auto club that gave roadside service. And she'd never changed a tire in her life. Shannon slowly climbed out of the truck and examined the deflated right front tire. There were many things she'd never contemplated doing before Rob had assaulted her. Changing a tire should be a piece of cake.

"NEED SOME HELP?"

Shannon looked back over her shoulder in alarm at the driver of the blue sedan that had pulled up behind her. She'd been so intent on figuring out how the jack worked and at the same time soothing Samantha, who was mewling with growing indignation at being confined to her car seat, that she hadn't heard a car approach.

She gazed up warily at the brown-haired man who'd offered his assistance. He had a hard dangerous look to his face, or what she could see of his face beneath the reflective sunglasses concealing his eyes. Something about the sharply chiseled nose and the shadow of stubble clinging to his jaw made her throat go dry as she rose from her crouched position. "Thank you for offering," she said firmly over the sound of Samantha's distressed cries, "but I'm sure I can manage. It's the twenty-first century. Women change tires. I'm setting a good example for my daughter."

The man laughed dryly and removed his sunglasses, clipping them onto the ribbed neck of his navy T-shirt. "She's a little young, wouldn't you say? It'd really be no trouble to help you, ma'am. The least I could do is drive into town and call someone to assist you. My name's Luke Mathews." Quiet intense gray-blue eyes gazed back at her. Pulled at her in a curious way Shannon didn't understand.

"Thank you, but it'd be faster to change the tire

than wait for a tow—'' she broke off as Samantha let out an eardrum-piercing wail. Shannon instinctively turned toward the truck and her daughter. Samantha's face was red and tear-streaked. Shannon reached through the open window and stroked her sticky cheek. ''Oh, Samantha, it's all right, baby. We'll be home soon.''

Samantha's mouth opened, her little pink tonsils quivering, and her eyes squeezed tight as another pitiful wail erupted from her tiny body.

Shannon's heart clutched at her daughter's obvious discomfort. Over the noise of her daughter's cries, she heard the engine of the sedan suddenly extinguish and a car door open. She looked back over her shoulder, alarmed to see Luke Mathews striding purposefully toward her truck.

''Ma'am,'' he said, a smile tugging at the corners of his lean mouth. His eyes were lit with a deference that inexplicably soothed her apprehension at his approach. ''It looks to me like you've already got your hands full. Why don't you take your baby out of your vehicle—it's safer and she'll be cooler—while I change the tire? It'll only take me a few minutes. Have you already set the emergency brake?''

Shannon decided Samantha's women's-lib training could take place another time. Right now her baby needed to be held and comforted. And her instincts were telling her that Luke Mathews didn't mean her or her daughter any harm. Not with those eyes.

''Yes, I set the brake,'' she replied as she jerked the door open to unbuckle Samantha's car seat. Her usually meek daughter's arms and legs waved in a fury as Shannon pulled her into her arms. Shannon grabbed her keys and her purse—just in case her instincts about Luke were wrong.

Shannon rocked Samantha in her arms as Luke popped the hubcap off the wheel and used some weird-looking tool to loosen the nuts slightly. Then he put the jack in place and began pumping the tire iron with practiced ease. The front right corner of the truck rose steadily off the ground.

"Are you a mechanic?" she asked, watching the smooth play of muscles rippling beneath his T-shirt. He wore faded jeans and scuffed running shoes.

"No, I've worked in construction mostly...well, until recently."

That explained the muscles that bulged in his arms like rocks. "Recently?"

"I was working for my brother-in-law's company in Vancouver. But he and my sister are going through a bitter divorce, and I didn't like being caught in the middle. He was cheating on her."

Shannon didn't know what to say except, "I'm sorry."

"I am, too. They've got kids." He nodded at the illustrations painted on her truck advertising her Garden Patch collection. "You in business for yourself?"

"Yes, I am. Sorry, I didn't introduce myself. I'm Mary Calder. I'm a crafter, mostly wooden crafts—letter boxes, birdhouses, yard ornaments and other home accent pieces."

Luke's smile as he glanced at her warmed her with frank admiration. "Good for you. I've been thinking about starting up my own custom-finish carpentry business—you know, molding, cabinetry. I've taken a few months off to scout out possibilities.'' Luke expertly finished loosening the nuts and slid off the damaged tire.

Shannon noticed his face turn serious, his lips pressing into a thin line as he examined the puncture. ''What is it?'' she asked, coming closer to peer over his shoulder.

He showed her a four-inch-long slit. ''There's your trouble.''

Shannon sighed. ''And they're new tires. Maybe I can have it repaired under the warranty.''

Luke didn't say anything. He put the damaged tire in the truck bed and hoisted the spare into his arms.

Shannon tried not to stare at the flexed muscles in his arms. She couldn't remember ever being fascinated by her ex-husband's physique. Or was it that ever since Rob had hit her, she was more aware of the threat a man's physical strength imposed? She pushed the disturbing thought away and focused on what Luke had just told her about his employment situation. An idea took form in her mind. ''I don't suppose you'd be interested in a part-time job while you're scouting out those possibilities?'' She went on quickly, feeling heat climb into her cheeks. ''I'm looking for a woodworker to cut the shapes I need for my crafts. With your experience it sounds like you're well qualified. I'm not sure I can pay you what you usually make doing construction, but it would be something while you're trying to decide what to do with your future.''

His gaze flickered up to meet hers, steady and soothing as the dusky skies of twilight. He didn't ap-

pear the least bit offended by her spontaneous offer.
Shannon wondered if those eyes ever ignited into a
rage. When she'd fallen in love with Rob, she'd never
imagined that he would hurt her, either. An event-
planning consultant, Rob had always seemed confident
and in control. The type of person corporations and
organizations depended on to flawlessly carry off their
conferences and special events down to the last detail.
But Shannon hadn't been able to depend on him to
cherish her as a husband should cherish his wife.

Still, she told herself reasonably, she wasn't asking
Luke to share her life—only work for her part-time.
Shannon clutched Samantha tightly to her hip and held
her breath. Would Luke accept her offer?

HOOK, LINE AND SINKER, she'd offered him a job.
Luke's mouth pulled into a slow halfhearted grin that
made him feel hollow inside as he pretended to mull
over her offer. What the hell was the matter with him?
He was unofficially working a murder investigation.
His *wife's* murder investigation. He should feel
pleased that the suspect had swallowed his background
story and offered him a job. Instead, he felt deeply ill
at ease.

The Mary Tatiana Calder he'd been conversing with
for the past fifteen minutes didn't strike him as being
a hardened criminal who'd stolen a woman's identity
to defraud a bank. Not with that fresh face, the pristine
eyelet top and those comfortably faded jeans. On the
surface she seemed like the kind of frank warmhearted
woman the world depended on to raise children, run
countless errands and volunteer for good causes, in

addition to being loving wives and career women. But even nice women with soft beguiling smiles, legs a model would envy and gently rounded derrieres had secrets. This Mary was a paradox.

Her truck's tire had been deliberately punctured—probably with a knife when he was inside the hardware store. She was lucky that she and her daughter hadn't had an accident.

Why would someone want to harm her?

Mary was patiently waiting for his reply. "I just might take you up on your offer," he said finally as he methodically tightened another nut. "Might be nice to have something to keep me busy until I make some decisions—and I have to admit my hands are aching to hold some tools." He glanced at her again, letting his eyes tangle with her hazel ones over her baby's silken head as long as he dared. Those hazel eyes spelled trouble. They were like the surface of a lake—shimmering with sunlight one minute, clouded with some inner torment the next. "I left my toolbelt at home—a definite mistake."

"You can borrow my toolbelt if you take the job," she said with a teasing lilt to her voice. "When would you be willing to start?"

Luke felt himself erecting an invisible wall to block out the wholesome appeal of her personality. "When would you like me to start?" he countered, matching her tone.

"Is tomorrow too soon? That would give me a chance to check your references this afternoon."

Ah, references. So, she wasn't as gullible as he'd first assumed. At least he hadn't been lying about his carpentry experience. He'd spent a few summers in his youth doing construction for a friend's father's business, and he'd been renovating the eighty-year-old fixer-upper he and Mary had bought to raise the family they'd hoped to have.

"I don't have a résumé," he admitted. "I'm staying at the Orchard Inn in Oliver, but if you give me your number, I could call you later with the information."

The baby's eyelids drooped heavily as her head fitted snugly against her mother's shoulder. As Mary lovingly cupped her head, an S-shaped frown settled between Mary's brows. "How about I call you, instead?" she suggested. "Samantha's schedule is a little unpredictable. Could you get together at least three references by five tonight?"

"No problem," Luke assured her, wondering if her guardedness over her phone number was prompted by plain common sense—or fear. She wasn't wearing a wedding band. Was she a woman living alone? Maybe her relationship with the baby's father hadn't worked out. Luke mulled over the ramifications of this possibility in his mind. She'd listed only the post-office-box address in the ad she'd posted in the hardware store. "You can reach me at the motel." He told her the room number as he finished tightening the last nut.

A flush of color touched her lightly freckled cheeks like the blush of sun-ripened apricots, making him aware once again how different she was from his Mary. His wife's skin had been like milk and honey in the winter, the honey tones darkening to bronze in the sun. And when she was flustered or angry, twin scarlet blossoms stained her cheeks.

Grief swelled in him.

"Sounds like we're close to a deal, then," she said in a tone that sounded too open and sweetly sensual to be businesslike. Or criminal.

Luke swore to himself and struggled to maintain an impersonal professional distance. "Y-yes, ma'am."

She smiled down at him as he disengaged the jack. "You can call me Mary."

Mary.

"Sure M—" Luke straightened, the jack in his hand, towering above her by a good six inches. His jaw tightened rebelliously, refusing to produce the name he'd said thousands of times. But never like this. Never in a moment of deceit.

Mary took an unconscious step backward, wariness rising in the dappled-hazel depths of her eyes like plumes of smoke. Luke realized swiftly that he was blowing it. "Sure, Mary," he said more forcefully than he intended. A dirty feeling coated his insides.

Mary trembled. And Luke wondered if his distaste for saying her name had shown. Or was she afraid of something or someone else? Had she realized that tire hadn't slit itself? He pretended to misinterpret her shudder. "Your arms are shaking. Is your daughter growing heavy?" Before she could object, he opened the truck's passenger door so she could buckle Samantha in her car seat. Luke stepped away from the door and stowed the jack.

Arms free again, Mary turned to him and offered him her hand and a smile of gratitude. Neither of which Luke felt comfortable about accepting.

"Thank you, Luke. This probably sounds like a cliché, but you rescued me today in more ways than one. I'll give you a call about five at your motel, okay?''

''I'll be expecting it.'' For several seconds Luke's thoughts scattered at the sensation Mary's hand created in his. Soft. Her hand felt so soft and delicately feminine. So…

Misleading.

That was the only term Luke would allow himself to describe his intense reaction to her touch. He released her fingers quickly, feeling as if his response betrayed his wife in some fundamental way.

As Mary climbed into her truck and drove off with a smile and a wave, Luke couldn't help wondering what he was walking into and how it might be connected to his wife's murder. The truck's punctured tire had his gut instinct shrieking warnings that something wasn't right. Luke was afraid for Mary and her daughter.

Imposter or not, this Mary Calder, whoever she was, had an enemy.

Chapter Two

Shannon was deeply relieved when Luke's references all checked out. Even though the southern Okanagan wasn't exactly teeming with crime, it had been risky to allow a stranger to change her truck's flat tire. Even riskier to offer him a job out of the blue. But she'd taken all the right precautions by not giving Luke her phone number or home address until after she'd verified his references. She just hoped he would work out until she could find a more permanent replacement.

Luke's brother-in-law hadn't sounded pleased that Luke was taking on a part-time job. But the two clients who'd returned her calls last night had raved about his reliability and his finish work.

And Luke had been willing to start this morning. Surely it was the prospect of getting some work done this afternoon that made her heart race with anticipation when she heard his sedan pull into her drive right on time, wasn't it?

LUKE SHOWED UP for his first day on the job determined to make substantial headway into solving the mystery of Mary Calder. Yesterday after he'd made arrangements for his phony references, he'd checked her phone number and discovered she only had a business line listed under her company's name, not a residential one under her own name. Then he'd spent a half hour combing the listings for Calder in the phone book for Blossom Valley and the nearby towns, but none of the three Calders he'd dialed had acknowledged being related to Mary. However, one elderly gent had offered the information that Luke wasn't the only one who'd called seeking a woman by the same name.

Luke eyed dispassionately the tidy white cottage with crisp blue trim on the porch rails and the gray weatherbeaten detached garage, which were set back in a stand of trees. Two oak-barrel halves overflowing with salmon geraniums and mounds of white flowers marked the beginning of a stepping-stone path that wended its way to the cottage's front door. A patchy lawn, bare in spots, stretched down to the cattail-fringed shore of Kettle Lake.

Luke felt his body tense as he climbed out of the sedan. Somehow the prospect of seeing Mary again made him feel as if he was entering a war zone populated with more enemy troops than allies.

Mary emerged from the cottage as he reached the stone path. "Hi, Luke!" she called out. The welcoming sunny warmth of her smile hit him like a sharp blow to the ribs. Without the thirty pounds of equipment and body armor he usually wore while on duty, Luke felt exposed and vulnerable to the emotional rounds her every look and gesture seemed to inflict on him.

With her flaxen hair glinting in the sunlight and her lighthearted step, Mary looked the picture of innocence in blue-and-white candy-striped overall shorts and a white tank top. She wore red running shoes painted with black dabs that made each foot look like a wedge of watermelon, and white cotton socks edged with blue hand-crocheted lace. Luke dredged up a smile and tucked his thumbs into the front pockets of his jeans. A massive weight settled in his stomach as if he'd swallowed rocks for breakfast. Nothing was more important to him than finding out who had murdered his wife. "Hi yourself," he replied. "Nice day, isn't it?"

"It's beautiful. I just put Samantha down in her crib for her nap. If we're lucky she'll go to sleep, and I can give you an uninterrupted tour of my workshop. It's out here in the garage...."

She was babbling. Was he making her nervous? Or was she worried about the baby? Or the threat against her life yesterday? Luke noticed she carried a portable baby monitor in her hand. He fell into step beside her and tried to act casual as she led him to the detached garage. But he felt more awkward than an adolescent on a first date. Fortunately Mary was doing enough talking to carry both sides of the conversation.

She paused to unlock the door and flick on the overhead fluorescent lights. "I'm warning you, my workshop is small, but functional."

She wasn't exaggerating. Luke examined the collection of power tools she had skillfully crammed into the one-car garage, which was little more than a shack constructed of decaying cedar siding. At least it had a window, albeit a small one, to bring in some light and ventilation.

It wasn't every day he met a woman who knew a jigsaw from a scroll saw, much less wasn't afraid of the whine or the ten-inch gleaming blade of a miter saw. Luke was frankly impressed that this Mary Calder seemed totally in her element, ankle-deep in sawdust. His wife had always tiptoed into his workshop as if getting sawdust on her three-hundred-dollar shoes and tracking sawdust into the other parts of the house were indictable offenses.

But why would someone want to hurt this Mary?

Luke detected an unmistakable wariness in her hazel eyes as she spoke to him, the same wariness he'd glimpsed fleetingly yesterday. It was the same hunted look perps wore when he questioned them on the street. Gut instinct told him there was something lurking here behind Mary's bright smiles. He hoped, with time, that he could convince her to share her fears. Meanwhile, he'd provide protection for her and her daughter. Not that he was armed. Only federal police officers could transport firearms from one province to another.

As she opened a cupboard to show him where she stored her reversible electrical drill and bits, Luke could hear via the monitor Samantha noisily sucking on a bottle.

"Are these your husband's tools?" he asked mildly. He had noted the absence of a wedding band yesterday when he was changing the truck's tire.

She looked startled. "No. They're all mine. I took up crafting after Samantha's father died."

"I'm sorry."

She waved away his sympathy with a flustered smile, setting the baby monitor on the workbench beside a plastic file box filled with manila files. She pulled some patterns from two of the files. "Basically I've got forty-plus designs in my Garden Patch collection that I sell to retailers in the area. About half my designs are seasonal items. My busiest periods are Christmas, Halloween and Easter, though business is brisk in the summer with the tourists. The files here contain all the patterns you'll be using. The patterns clearly indicate how many pieces must be cut per finished item. And I usually make a note on the inside of the file folder how many pieces can be cut from a particular dimension of lumber." She pointed to a pile of lumber stacked on a couple of sawhorses. "These pine one-by-eights are for a rush order of letter boxes and welcome signs." She laid the patterns out on two of the planks, her quick fingers minutely adjusting the placement of each pattern piece. "I'll need a dozen signs and eight letter boxes as soon as possible."

Luke slid his hand over the surface of the raw wood and tried not to be so aware of the scent of this woman, like an exotic hothouse flower, mingling with the aroma of the sawdust and the cedar shingles as she positioned a pattern piece along the grain of the wood. He'd hung up his toolbelt and sold the house when Mary had died, afraid that he might destroy, rather than create, in his grief. Finishing the house would have been a constant reminder of all that he'd lost. The condo he lived in now, with its neutral color scheme and barren walls, was blessedly free of memories of Mary. Someday Luke thought he might hang pictures on the walls and empty some of the boxes that filled the spare bedroom. "I think I can handle that."

She nodded approvingly. "You'll find sandpaper in a plastic bin beneath the workbench. I'd like the pieces sanded and ready for finishing. I do most of the painting in the house." She paused awkwardly, her face blanching beneath the smattering of freckles. "You're welcome to come inside to use the facilities, have a coffee. I always keep a pot on. Since we're a ways out of town, you might want to bring a lunch and keep it in the refrigerator."

"Thank you."

Shannon hoped she was doing a good job of hiding her nervousness. Even though she'd checked Luke's references and knew he was who and what he purported himself to be, warning twinges ignited inside her like firecrackers when they'd stepped into the garage. He was so male. So tall. And those competent blunt-tipped fingers had seemed so large as he'd stroked her tools.

Shannon told herself she was being ridiculous. She couldn't live in fear of every man who entered her life.

Her ex-husband had robbed her of too much already. She wasn't going to give him the power to make her distrust Luke. It was perfectly reasonable to allow Luke inside the garage and access to her home to use the washroom.

She tilted her head and caught his unwavering gray-blue gaze. "Are you going to be staying at the Orchard

Inn in Oliver for the time being? I'd like to know where I can reach you. Sometimes no matter how hard I try to keep to a schedule, something happens to throw me off.''

''Are there any motels in Blossom Valley? That would save me some driving time.''

''There's one motel outside of town, though it's usually full this time of year because it's on the highway. It might be more affordable for you to rent a place by the week. I can guarantee you steady part-time work for the next two weeks—it'll take me at least that long to find someone permanent. You can ask at the tourist-info center in town for a list of local rentals, or you might try asking Bill Oakes. I rent this place from him. He owns the blue house with the butterflies as you turned onto Shady Pines Road. Prices are reasonable because it's not on one of the more popular lakes. The cottages along this road belong to his family, most of whom have moved to other parts of Canada. They don't want to sell, it seems, so Bill rents them out and calls the place Shady Pines Resort.''

Those blue-gray eyes regarded her thoughtfully. ''Thanks. I'll keep that in mind. I take it you're not from around here, either? Your accent sounds more Eastern.''

Shannon blinked. ''Who me? No I—''

A cry pierced the air in the garage, followed by a thump and a plaintive wail.

Shannon gave Luke an apologetic smile. ''I'm sorry, Luke, I have to go.'' Before he could say a word, Shannon hightailed it out of the garage.

Luke stared after Mary, his mind churning with speculation. She'd been frustratingly evasive when it came to answering personal questions. Was she truly a widow or was she lying?

He'd bet coffee and a doughnut she was lying. Had the person who'd slit her tire been an ex-spouse angered over a custodial dispute? Or was there more to it than that? Had she taken her daughter without the father's consent? That might explain why she'd stolen another woman's identity, if she had. But Luke had no proof that this Mary Calder wasn't whom she claimed—only unscientific hunches.

Luke studied the pattern pieces she'd arranged on the pine board, then rearranged them to make a better fit. Somehow he'd make all the pieces of this case fit together, one at a time.

When, suddenly he heard Mary's voice in the garage, speaking in soothing tones to the baby, Luke realized she had forgotten to take the baby monitor with her. "Oh, Samantha, come here, baby," she crooned. "It's okay. Everything's all right. Mommy's going to take care of you. Always."

Was it Luke's imagination or did he detect an air of desperation in her voice?

SHANNON WAS IMPRESSED when Luke brought her a stack of the finished wood for the welcome signs at the end of the afternoon.

"This ought to get you started," he said with a gruff smile that made her chest feel strangely tight as she opened the screen door to him. "I'll do the letter boxes tomorrow." His face was beaded with a fine film of perspiration, and his clothes were speckled with saw-dust. And he looked sexier than a pinup boy in a tux-edo. Raw and elemental.

Shannon took a firm grip of her hormones and reached down to scoop up Samantha, who was chew-ing on a biscuit. She'd had a productive afternoon. She'd painted two-dozen crow plant pokes. Tonight she could start on the welcome signs. "You look hot, Luke. Could I offer you a cold drink? Iced tea? Soda?"

"Water will be fine, thank you."

Shannon motioned toward her worktable. "You can put the signs there and have a seat at the counter. Feel free to wash your hands at the sink if you like."

He nodded wordlessly. As he stepped into her cot-tage, what she had always considered an airy space seemed to shrink enough to barely encompass his shoulders. Shannon fought the ripples of panic swell-ing in her.

Forcing a bright smile, she marched to the refrig-erator and yanked open the door, reaching inside for a pitcher of water. One-handed, she poured him a drink and circled to the other side of the counter before presenting it to him. She felt safer with the width of the counter between them. But as he sat down across from her and she met his gaze, she could have sworn he understood her actions. Shame seared her. Was she that transparent?

Luke noted Mary's uneasiness and the emotions shifting in her eyes, as well as the pink tide of color that rose from her neck and seeped into her cheeks before she turned away from him to examine his work.

With her head lowered and her body pressed against the table as she held her daughter protectively on her hip, she reminded him of a hunted animal burrowing into its surroundings to escape the notice of a passing predator.

Compassion squeezed his heart. Just what or who was she running from?

He took a sip of water and let his gaze travel around the room. It exuded the whimsical touches of Mary's creativity. Wreaths, bouquets of dried flowers and dozens of decorative hand-painted crafts dangled from pegs. Pegged racks painted a country blue were mounted at eye level on the pine-paneled walls. On one wall a narrow shelf was installed above the rack and held an assembly line of crafts in various stages of completion. Pencils, markers and brushes were carefully arranged in glass canning jars on the cottage's dining table—an antique harvest table waxed to a soft mellow gleam—that obviously served as her worktable. A pine cupboard wedged into a corner held small plastic bottles of acrylic paint and cans of stain and varnish.

On the other side of the table was a playpen filled with stuffed toys and activity sets. He couldn't see any photos of family and friends. No deceased husband. Like him, had she put the photos away because the memories they evoked were too painful? The room perfectly summed up what he already knew of Mary's life: work, motherhood and a blank past.

He watched her run a finger along the sanded edge of a sign. "These look great, Luke," she said, glancing back at him over her shoulder. "Expertly cut. Perfectly sanded. I'll be begging you to stay on permanently if you keep this up.''

Luke was oddly pleased by her compliment. It had felt good to see the shapes emerge from the wood. ''Thanks, but don't get your hopes up. We both agreed this was temporary. I took the liberty of looking at some of the other patterns. I like your designs. How long have you been doing this?''

She shrugged. ''Oh, I've been designing and painting things for years. I finally decided to be brave and turn my hobby into a job.''

Her breezy reply was characteristically vague. Luke dug in his heels, determined to peel back a layer or two. ''I admire your initiative. It must not be easy running a business and being a single mom.''

He saw the muscles in the arm that circled her daughter tighten perceptibly. Still hovering over the worktable, she plucked a paintbrush from a jar, examined the bristles as if checking to make sure it was clean, then tucked it back into the jar. ''It hasn't been easy,'' she admitted faintly, her back still to him. ''When I was a teenager complaining about homework and studying, my mother used to tell me that if it wasn't hard, then it wasn't worth doing.'' She turned toward him fully, her eyes glowing with steely determination. ''I didn't understand what she meant until I started this business. Now I'm glad my mother made me pay attention to algebra and geometry.''

Luke laughed dryly. Samantha stopping chewing on her biscuit at the deep unfamiliar sound and looked at him in sudden interest, her delicate bow-shaped brows lifting as if questioning what her mother was doing conversing with this strange man in their home. Luke gave her an amused grin.

"She's a cutie. How old is she?"

"Almost ten months."

"She's walking early. My brother's kids were closer to a year old when they started walking. His son could crawl up bookcases and cabinets."

"Thankfully Samantha isn't that adventurous. She never quite got the hang of crawling, but I think her natural curiosity to touch things out of her arm's reach propelled her into standing, then walking. She loves brightly colored objects, especially flowers. Right, baby?"

Eyes gleaming, Samantha gave her mother and Luke a coquettish smile.

Luke laughed. "I'll bet she just likes mischief. With a smile like that, she's going to break a lot of hearts when she hits high school," he predicted.

"You think?" Mary laughed and playfully dabbed at a splotch of drool on her daughter's chin. "I hope she has more teeth by the time she hits high school."

Luke took a stab at shifting the conversation to the more personal. "Did you go to high school here in Blossom Valley? Place doesn't look big enough to have a high school."

"There's a high school in one of the nearby towns."

Luke kept his smile steady despite the way she'd sidestepped his question. Again. "I'll bet you got all A's in art class. Is that where you learned to paint—in high school? Or did you major in art at university?"

"Actually I taught myself to paint from books and

magazines, then took a few craft classes. I was an administrative assistant before I decided to turn my hobby into a business. I have to say I much prefer being my own boss to being someone else's gofer.''

''What kind of company did you work for?''

''The government,'' she said with a dismissive wave of her hand as if all government offices were the same. ''It gave me a whole new perspective on office politics. Though I miss the regular paycheck. That's one thing you might want to keep in mind if you're going into business for yourself,'' she said pointedly.

''There's that,'' he agreed. ''I guess I'd miss my soon-to-be ex-brother-in-law and the rest of his crew. It must be isolating working for yourself.'' Luke took a sip of water, deliberately waiting to see if Mary picked up the thread and carried the conversation. Perhaps mention the department where she'd worked or the names of co-workers she missed or still kept in touch with. Anything that might help him confirm her identity.

Usually if you waited long enough, people felt obligated to fill silences.

And Luke was vitally aware that this Mary might have the answers that would fill the yawning silence in his heart. His gaze settled on her expectantly.

She moistened her lips. ''I'm too busy to feel isolated. Taking care of Samantha and keeping up with orders keeps me on my toes. Speaking of orders, what hours are you available tomorrow?'' she asked, rocking the baby on her hip. Dropping her gaze, she pulled a pencil from a jar, her expression all business as she examined the day planner open on the table.

She'd changed the subject so effectively Luke realized he couldn't push the topic any further today without raising her suspicions. But while he might have surrendered this minor skirmish, he wasn't going to lose the war. As Mary penciled in a four-hour shift on the calendar for the next day, he promised himself that someday soon, whether she liked it or not, he'd be downright intimate with her personal history.

BILL OAKES WAS HOME when Luke rang the bell beneath the faded sign reading Shady Pines Resort, Management. He was an elderly man with humped shoulders, elfin ears and a cheek-splitting grin that declared life still agreed with him. Or else he was showing off thousands of dollars worth of dentures, Luke mused.

The resort caretaker's shrewd brown eyes assessed Luke as he explained his desire to rent a cottage for two weeks and gave Mary Calder's name as a reference. "She's hired me to do some woodworking for her."

Bill Oakes nodded. "Mary's a nice girl. She repainted my butterflies for me." He gestured at five vibrantly painted wooden butterflies that looked as if they had just alighted on the blue siding of his residence. "My wife—God rest her soul—bought those for the cottage years ago. They were looking faded. I'm not good with paints and such, but Mary offered to do them for me. Didn't charge me a cent."

"She did a wonderful job," Luke said. "Has she been your tenant long?"

"Oh, let's see… A year ago last April. It was right

after her husband died. She needed a change, what with the baby coming and all.''

Luke quickly computed the dates. Mary had been murdered in March of that year, on St. Patrick's Day. ''Yes, she mentioned he'd died and that she wasn't from this area originally,'' he murmured conversationally, grateful that Mary had suggested there might be a cottage available for rent at the resort. Renting here could provide him with additional opportunities to find out more about the woman with his wife's name.

''She's got a mother and an aunt in the East, I believe,'' Bill Oakes said, withdrawing a ring of keys from his pocket. ''Now I do have a couple of cottages available for weekly or monthly arrangements. One's a lot nicer than the other. Come on, I'll give you a tour. We've got our own private beach.''

Luke waited for Bill Oakes to lock the front door, then walked with the elderly gentleman along a series of paths that wound from one lot to the next. Glimpses of Kettle Lake were visible through the trees, diamonds of sunlight dancing across its blue waters. Regaling Luke with tales of his six siblings, their children and grandchildren, Bill Oakes extolled the virtues of Shady Pine's sandy beach, then showed him the two available cottages.

Luke chose the smaller of the cottages, a drab decaying structure that boasted one bedroom the size of a janitor's closet and indoor plumbing. The furnishings smelled musty and damp, but it was a two-minute walk to Mary's cottage. And Bill didn't have any objection to his moving in that evening.

On his way to the motel to grab his luggage, Luke

mulled over the two kernels of information that Oakes had given him about Mary: she might originally be from the East, and she'd arrived in Blossom Valley a couple of weeks after his wife's murder. It wasn't much to work with, but combined with Mary's vagueness about her history and her coincidental resemblance to his wife, it opened the door wide to the possibility that there might be some connection between this woman and his wife's murder.

Luke's fingers tightened on the steering wheel as the unease that had lingered in his belly all day like an undigested meal rose sharply in his throat. Despite the steady wave of cool air blasting from the air conditioner, Luke broke out in a cold sweat. He'd arrested people from all walks of life and knew that almost anyone given enough motivation was capable of committing the most heinous of crimes. But the thought that this Mary Calder had been involved in such a brutal act sickened him. Slamming on the brakes, he pulled off the road and bounced onto the grassy shoulder of a peach orchard. A bell pinged repeatedly, reminding him he'd left his keys in the ignition as he climbed out of his rental car. He needed fresh air.

He gulped in two ragged breaths, then doubled over and vomited onto the freshly mown grass.

THE PHONE RANG at ten-thirty in the evening just as Mary was washing her paintbrushes. She'd finished the fine-detail work on the plant pokes and gotten a head start on the signs, but she was too tired to do more tonight. She quickly dried her hands on a paper towel and reached for the phone. Who could be calling her at this hour? Her mother and Aunt Jayne were in Halifax—in a time zone three hours ahead. And they always called from pay phones so Shannon's number couldn't show up on a phone bill.

Could it possibly be Luke Mathews calling to say he'd be late tomorrow or had changed his mind about working for her because she'd been such an idiot today?

Why did that thought make her experience a sharp pang of disappointment?

Because ever since she'd walked out on her marriage to Rob, she hadn't allowed herself to look twice at a handsome man, much less enjoy the simple pleasure of conversation. She'd been too focused on running and being safe. Even the eight months Rob had spent in prison after she'd pressed stalking charges against him, she'd been afraid to make new friends, afraid to share information about herself, worried that she might inadvertently give away her location or her new place of employment…and Rob would somehow find her again.

Even though she had Samantha, having Luke here today had made her painfully aware of how starved she was for friendship and adult company.

The phone rang again.

"Hello?" she said softly, breathlessly, into the receiver, her pulse spiking as an image of Luke, dusty and virile, unfolded in her mind.

Silence met her greeting. But the line hadn't gone dead. She could hear sounds in the background: the unmistakable clinking of cutlery.

"Hello," she repeated patiently, feeling the roots of

fear sink deep into her chest and twine around her heart. "Who's calling? What number are you trying to reach?"

The caller didn't respond. But she could still hear the noises.

Shannon hung up slowly, telling herself it was probably a wrong number, someone who'd misdialed and been confused by the sound of an unfamiliar voice. It couldn't possibly be Rob this time—even though it was the third wrong number she'd received this week. She shook her head firmly, ticking off on her fingers all the logical reasons it couldn't possibly be Rob. She'd taken all kinds of precautions—to the point of cutting off all contact with friends. Aunt Jayne and her mother didn't even have her new name or phone number written down out of fear the information might somehow end up in Rob's hands. They'd kept news of Samantha's birth private and didn't even keep photos of Samantha and Shannon at home. Instead, Shannon mailed them to a post-office box belonging to an acquaintance of her mother's—a bridge partner—who kept them in her home, no questions asked, so her mother could see them at her weekly bridge games. Shannon never included a return address, and the acquaintance had no idea of Shannon's new identity. She and Samantha were safe here.

Still, tonight's phone call disturbed Shannon.

Enough to keep her awake into the early hours of the morning.

Chapter Three

"Sorry I couldn't get back to you yesterday on the license plate. I was working on another unsolved murder," Detective Vaughn told Luke over the phone the next morning. His voice was brisk and merciless, like a wire brush scraping rusted metal. Luke heard the sounds of papers being leafed through in a file. "The truck is registered to Mary Tatiana Calder."

Luke grunted a noncommittal response. Hearing his wife's middle name spoken out loud by another human being rankled. It seemed a violation of the trust his wife had had in him. A secret only the two of them had shared. But there were no secrets from the police.

And this Mary Calder would have no secrets from him.

Luke brought the detective up to speed about the change in his accommodations and his interview with Bill Oakes. "He told me the suspect has been renting since a year ago last April—two weeks after Mary died. She told him her husband was dead, which is the same line she gave me."

Vaughn was silent a moment. "You think there's a custody issue involved?"

"Possibly. It makes the most sense to me. I didn't see any pictures of a man when I was in the house. I checked the garage for boxes of personal belongings, but no dice."

"So maybe the husband slit the tire?" Vaughn suggested. Luke could almost hear the gears churning in the detective's head. "That puts an interesting spin on the situation. You got a name for the husband?"

"No, not even a first name. But then, she's evasive whenever I ask personal questions. My gut feeling is she's running from something."

"Or someone. Think you can get her prints? We might be able to identify her. Stands to reason that if she was involved in Mary's murder or is the type to buy stolen ID, she may have been in trouble with the law before. She might have a record."

"I'll get them," Luke promised.

Vaughn instructed him to keep in touch and hung up.

Dressed in jeans and a T-shirt, with the small cell phone tucked into his pocket, Luke took the dirt path by the lake in the direction of Mary's cottage. She wasn't expecting him for another half hour, but he figured he could get the lay of the land and keep a vigilant eye on her cottage at the same time. The person who'd slit her tire might be keeping close tabs on her. And Luke didn't want anything to happen to Mary and her daughter. Mary was the key to the answers he needed.

Voices drifted over to him from the other cottages. But the only person he encountered on the path was a sullen-faced teen in a black tank top and baggy swimming trunks that hung past his knees. The kid had bleached his dark hair to an electrifying hue and had affixed a row of silver studs to his right earlobe. Luke wondered if he'd ever looked that sullen as a teen.

Mary and Samantha were outside when he arrived. Samantha was sitting in a small sandbox with brightly colored toys while Mary was seated in a blue Adirondack chair that someone—Mary herself?—had turned into a work of art with hand-painted renderings of garden spades, hoes and seed packets. A mug of coffee sat on the wooden arm of the chair and a pencil and sketchbook were in her lap.

"Good morning, Luke, you're right on time." Mary's welcoming smile was so cheerful and beguiling it stirred a response from his body that was far too vigorous for his comfort. She was dressed in a pair of sky-blue shorts this morning, with a matching blouse.

He averted his gaze from the devastating eyeful of tanned silky arms and legs as a razor-sharp sliver of guilt pricked his heart. "Of course I'm on time. Believe it or not, I know a number of contractors and subcontractors who actually show up at the time they promise."

Mary laughed doubtfully.

Telling himself that he wasn't attracted to her but to her passing resemblance to his Mary, didn't help. It only made him feel more unsure. The truth was he didn't want to feel anything for this Mary and her daughter. He was here to seek justice for his wife, nothing more, nothing less. He needed closure and peace to free himself from the limbo of his existence. Then maybe he could get on with his life.

Samantha gave a whimper of frustration as she tried to turn over a mold filled with sand. Luke hunkered down beside her so he could see her face beneath the brim of her pink sun hat and smiled at the unidentifiable clumps of sand she'd created in the sandbox. Judging by the forms she was playing with, they were supposed to be animal shapes. "I see you're quite the designer, kid, following in your mother's footsteps. Want some help making that turtle?"

Samantha sweetly handed him another shovel, those big smoky brown eyes of hers a trap in themselves. Luke helped her fill the plastic turtle mold with sand, then flipped it over. The turtle held its shape. Samantha clapped her hands as he added two tiny pinecone eyes. "There you go, kid."

An unbearable ache wedged just below his heart, widening into a chasm of pain deep enough to drown in. It took every ounce of his willpower not to let himself think about what kind of father he might have been if he and his wife had had a baby. He'd been eagerly doing his duty to get her pregnant in the weeks before her death.

The Adirondack chair creaked behind him, and Mary's voice, rich with motherly indulgence, encircled him in a bubble of intimacy that touched the emptiness inside him. "Oops, what are you going to do with that pinecone, Samantha?" she said as her daughter pinched another pinecone between her thumb and forefinger and ever so carefully placed it off-center on the turtle's head for a nose.

"Nice touch, Samantha," he praised her, patting her back awkwardly. "Every turtle needs a nose. It helps them find lunch.'' Samantha giggled as Luke rose and brushed his hands on his jeans.

He risked taking another look at Mary and tried not to think about all those seemingly insignificant yet cherished moments he'd spent with his wife. The Saturday-morning French-toast breakfasts, the visits to antique shops to find just the right touches for their home. The hello and goodbye kisses. So many lost moments, lost dreams. So much he owed his wife. Luke took a firm mental step away from the edge of the chasm that threatened to suck him into its darkness. He could do this no matter what it took.

To his relief, Mary wasn't paying him any mind. She was scanning the drive and the lawn leading down to the lake, the S-shaped frown he'd noticed yesterday inching between her brows. ''Hey, I just noticed you're on foot this morning. Did someone drop you off?''

''No, my car's parked at my cottage down the way. Bill Oakes had a vacancy, so I moved in last night.''

''Oh, I thought maybe you were visiting the area with a friend you hadn't mentioned.'' Luke groaned inwardly at the hint of interest in her voice. Was she subtly inquiring whether he was involved in a relationship? It was bad enough that he felt some feelings of attraction for Mary. He didn't want them to be reciprocated—even if it might facilitate getting some answers out of her! The situation was complicated enough. ''I'm staying here alone,'' he admitted finally, figuring the less he elaborated, the better.

She flashed him another beguiling smile. ''That's great you got a cottage. Which one?''

"Small one, in terrible need of repair. I've heard trains that were quieter than the pipes knocking in the walls when the shower's turned on. But the price was right."

"That's Abner's cottage. The oldest brother. He's tightfisted, apparently. Can't see why he should spend good money on improvements for other people to enjoy."

Luke studied her closely as she took a sip of coffee. Hair framed her face in tousled disarray as if she'd combed it with her fingers when she'd risen from bed. She wasn't wearing any makeup. There were lavender smudges under her eyes. From fear? Sleeplessness? Pushing herself too hard? "Bill Oakes didn't mention it," he said.

"Can I get you some coffee?" She started to rise.

He waved her to stay seated. "I'll get it. You keep working. Mugs are in the cupboard above the sink, right?"

Luke saw uncertainty flash in her eyes. Why? At the prospect of him entering her home?

She settled herself back into her chair. "Yes, help yourself. Sugar's in a bowl on the counter and there's cream in the fridge."

Luke nodded and ambled toward the front door. Conscious of the ticking seconds, his steps quickened once he'd stepped inside the cottage. The phone was mounted on the wall at the end of the kitchen counter. An old white pitcher crammed with pencils and a notepad was positioned near the phone, but there was none of the daily minutiae he expected to find: an address book, a calendar, letters, bills, bank statements. The day planner she'd had yesterday was nowhere in sight.

He quietly eased open the cupboard doors and the drawers nearest the phone. They held craft supplies and mismatched dishes. He surveyed the kitchen, dining and living areas for her purse, but didn't see it. Her worktable was covered with partially painted signs, but no files or books that might contain business records. Luke decided she probably kept her purse and her business records in her bedroom, out of her daughter's reach. Maybe she had a computer.

He'd have to find another opportunity to look. Luke found a mug and filled it with coffee. He noticed there weren't any photographs stuck to the refrigerator when he took out the cream. Not even a picture of Samantha. Luke found that odd. Most people who had kids plastered their homes with photos of their offspring.

As he stepped back outside, coffee in hand, he complimented Samantha on her progress at making a second turtle. Samantha beamed up at him, her eyes sparkling with mischief beneath the brim of her hat as she tipped over the mold. Sand spilled out and formed two mounds that looked more like a snowman than a turtle. Samantha giggled.

''Uh, oh,'' Luke said, not the least bit fooled by her attempt to entice him to play with her some more. He glanced back over his shoulder at Mary. ''Your daughter's pretty cute. She has your nose, but the rest of her must be her father.''

''She definitely has her father's eyes. The rest...I don't know, but I'll keep her just the way she is.''

Mary's reply was characteristically vague, but her face glowed with motherly pride.

"Did you name her after her father?"

"No, I've just always liked the name Samantha. You're good with her. She's usually shy around men. Especially when I take her to the doctor."

"It doesn't matter what age you are, you don't like doctors poking at you." Luke took a sip of his coffee. The conversation had the level of intimacy he wanted if he hoped to get Mary to open up to him, but he could feel her skating around the edges of his questions about her husband as if aware danger lurked beneath them. "What did your husband do?" he asked.

A shadow darted across her expressive eyes. She tilted her head to one side, the sunlight striking her hair and turning it to corn silk as she met his gaze directly. "I know you're just making conversation so we can get to know each other, but I'd rather not talk about my husband. He…" She paused, her lips twisting into a rueful smile. "It's hard to explain, but losing him taught me how important it is to live life in the here and now and live it to the fullest." As she spoke her shoulders squared as if threaded with an iron rod. "The past is over, done with, you can't change it— sometimes you can't even explain it. And the future, well, the future is something everyone assumes they'll have, but the truth is that the only sure moment we have is the right now. For me, that's my daughter and my business and the letter boxes that need to be cut today."

"Is that your subtle way of telling me to quit jawing and get to work?" Luke quipped, feeling a wave of admiration for her, even though she'd just firmly barred the door on further questions about her husband.

"Yes." The smile she gave him was pure, sweet and undeniably flirtatious. Luke promptly forgot about the past, the future and the need to cut the letter boxes in the present. The only thought on his mind in the here and now was that she had the most beautiful face, freckles, violet smudges and all. And those lips...would they feel as warm and sweet as the woman they belonged to?

Mary dug a key from the pocket of her shorts and handed it to him. "I hate to disturb Samantha when she's happy in the sand. Can you unlock the garage and pass me the key before you leave for the day?"

"Sure. I'll get started on the letter boxes right away." Their fingers brushed lightly as he accepted the key, and Luke felt his limbs tingle with a slow anticipatory heat that made him patently aware, once again, of how delicate and feminine she was and how long it had been since he'd held a woman in his arms.

But he'd never hold this woman in his arms. Over time, even the best liars slipped up. And Luke had all the time in the world when it came to finding out Mary's true identity.

CONCEALED BEHIND THE TREES, he watched them talking in front of her cottage. Anger rippled through him at the way she smiled at the man, as if she had no reason to be afraid. As if she didn't deserve to be punished. Did she think having a man around would protect her from him?

No one could protect her from him. He was too smart. He'd proved last night that he could rattle her whenever he wanted. He'd heard the fear in her voice when she'd answered the phone. He was in control.

And that was only just the beginning.

WITH LUKE NEARBY in the garage, Shannon felt undeniably safer than she had last night after that unsettling phone call. She felt protected in the same way she had when she was a child learning to ride a bike without training wheels, and her father had walked beside her, a hand ready to catch her bike and steady her should she need it. After the way Luke had come to her aid yesterday, she knew that if Rob suddenly turned up on her doorstep, she could trust Luke to help her.

Not that she could tell Luke everything. It was highly improbable that the phone call last night had been Rob, but she'd learned the hard way never to underestimate what her ex-husband was capable of doing. Shannon tried to concentrate on sketching the design for a scarecrow crafted from a four-by-four recycled fence post, but even the slightest movement in the trees surrounding the cottage set her on edge.

Her experience with Rob had made her paranoid, and the only effective way to deal with it was to acknowledge the fear as a self-protective instinct and let it ride itself out. A few weeks from now the phone call would be just another insignificant wrong number. In the meantime, she'd be vigilant as always.

Samantha, who was practicing her new walking skills, toddled unsteadily around the sandbox, babbling to her toys like an excited bird. Her round face was damp with perspiration from the rising heat of the morning sun. Shannon decided to give up all pretense of working. "You look hot, baby. Let's go inside and get you some juice."

As she leaned down to place her sketchbook on the grass at her feet, something whizzed past her head. A second later, it struck the big terra-cotta pot she'd planted with petunias and alyssum with a sharp crack, putting a ding in the pot.

Shannon stared at the object. It was a rock the size of a golf ball. If she hadn't bent over, it would have hit her in the head. It could have killed Samantha.

Panic spilled through her like carbonated bubbles. "Luke! Come quick!" she screamed as she leaped toward her daughter and scooped her up in her arms. A second missile hit the sandbox, spewing up sand inches from the spot where Samantha had been playing. "Stop it! You'll hurt someone," Shannon yelled as she ran toward the safety of their cottage, every cell in her body determined to protect her daughter. She yanked open the screen door, pulled it quickly closed behind her and secured the lock, her heart threatening to leap into her throat with every breath.

Samantha started to cry.

"Hush," Shannon whispered. She peered through the screen, scanning the foliage to determine from which direction the rocks had been thrown. *Please, God, don't let it be Rob.* The terror of the months he'd stalked her flared in her mind, a recurring nightmare that never left her. The phone calls. The notes filled with pleas, promises, threats and reminders of the vows she'd made to him, which she'd find on her windshield or taped to the door of her office building so that everyone at work could see. Or worse, the love notes he'd given her during her courtship that she'd find in the pockets of her clothes in her new dwellings. The cold dread that had hovered in the background of her every waking moment at the knowledge that she might turn around when she was walking down the street or purchasing groceries or heading for a meeting and find him watching her.

To her relief, Luke came tearing out of the garage, legs and arms pumping like a seasoned athlete.

"Mary? Where are you?"

Shannon had never been so glad to see muscles before. Surely Luke's construction-honed physique was intimidation enough to make whoever had thrown the rocks think twice before doing something so irresponsibly dangerous again.

"We're inside," she called back, hating the fear that invaded her voice. Hating the fact that she couldn't stop herself from leaping to the conclusion that Rob had somehow found her. "Someone just threw a couple of rocks at me and Samantha. One's by the planter. I was sitting in the chair, and it came from behind and hit the planter. It almost got me. The other one landed in the sandbox."

"Stay inside. I'll check it out."

Shannon's heart ricocheted in her chest as Luke took one look at the planter and the chair where she'd been sitting, then ran toward the trees. Seconds later, his navy T-shirt and jeans were swallowed up by shadows and bristly pine branches. She didn't want to think what might have happened if he hadn't been here. What if the first rock had struck her and knocked her unconscious? Or the second rock had hit Samantha?

Caution curbed Luke's movements as he skirted a thicket of chokecherry, searching for signs of Mary and Samantha's attacker, scanning the trees and scattered clumps of vegetation for movement and listening for sounds of snapped twigs. What the hell had just happened? This second incident on the heels of the slit tire two days before confirmed that Mary and her daughter were in real danger. From whom? Did this Mary know something about his wife's killer and someone wanted to silence her? His hair rose on the back of his neck. The stand of pine and aspen was eerily silent—no sound of birds chirping, making him think that someone was still nearby. Watching. Waiting.

"I know you're there," he said in an authoritative tone. "Come on out and apologize. That was a really stupid thing to do. Someone could have been seriously hurt."

Silence met his demand.

"Well, if you won't come to me, then I'll come to you." He strode toward a point in the path strewn with embedded stones, presuming the thrown rocks had originated there. Sure enough, two indentations in the sandy soil exposing fresh dirt confirmed his theory. He glanced in the direction of Mary's cottage. The only thing visible from this position was the roof. Had a kid decided to use the roof as a target? He examined the ground carefully for footprints or items that might have tumbled from a pocket when the culprit had run off. The ground was hard-packed and sprinkled with a layer of dry pine needles.

He jogged down the path in a direction away from Mary's cottage. There was no one in sight. Still, he continued on to the nearest cottage, where a man in a damp bathing suit, a bad sunburn ringing his neck, was pouring a bag of charcoal into a hibachi. Three kids ranging in age from maybe four to fourteen were fighting over a bag of hot dogs and a plate of buns.

Luke stopped to ask the man if he'd seen anyone pass by on the path in the last few minutes.

"Sorry. We were in the cottage," the man replied.

"All of you?"

"Yes."

Luke thanked him and returned to the path this time following it past Mary's cottage toward the private beach. Half-a-dozen families were enjoying the water and the sandy shore. A tanned elderly woman in a black bathing suit and wide-brimmed straw hat looked up from the pages of a magazine as he approached.

She gave him a measuring glance when he asked if anyone had arrived at the beach in the past few minutes. "I don't think so." She paused. "You don't look familiar."

"I'm staying in Abner's cottage."

"Oh, yes, my brother, Bill, dropped by last night to say he'd rented the cottage to the new man working for Mary Calder. Luke Mathews, isn't it? I'm Alice Nesbitt." She nodded toward the water. "Most of that unruly gang are my grandchildren. But I haven't seen Mary. Is that who you're looking for?"

Luke decided to level with the woman. Alice Nesbitt struck him as the kind of woman who'd make a useful ally. "Actually, someone threw a couple of rocks at Mary and her daughter a few minutes ago. Fortunately neither was injured, but I'd like to talk to whomever is responsible—make sure it doesn't happen again."

Alice's plain face showed shared concern. "I've been keeping an eye on the kids, and no one's left the beach. But I'll tell Bill what happened and have him go around to all the cottages and make it clear that kind of behavior isn't tolerated here. You're sure Mary and her baby weren't hurt?"

"They're fine. Mary's just shaken. I take it nothing like this has ever happened before?"

Alice didn't even hesitate. "Not that kind of trouble. Occasionally Bill catches groups of teens looking for uninhabited cottages to party in, but that's usually in the winter."

Luke was tempted to ask her about Mary, but he figured those kinds of questions would only get the woman's guard up. "Well, I'd better get back to work. Thanks for your help."

Luke hurried back to Mary's cottage, concern for Mary and her daughter's safety uppermost in his mind. They'd been the victims of two acts of malicious mischief in two days. Something was obviously going on here. Would this latest incident prompt Mary into confiding in him?

LUKE SEEMED to be gone forever. Shannon's fear had reached mammoth proportions by the time he returned, panting, a frown creasing his brow.

"I didn't see anybody," he said. "And neither did anyone in the next cottage or down at the beach. It was probably kids, goofing around. You likely scared them off when you screamed."

"You're sure it was kids? Did you see any footprints?"

His eyes narrowed on her, questioning. "Footprints?"

Shannon felt foolish. From his expression, she could tell she was behaving as paranoid as she felt.

Luke's hand settled on her shoulder, steadying her, making her long to lean into him until her fears quieted.

"I didn't see any footprints that would tell us for certain it was kids," he replied. "There are a lot of needles on the ground, and in some places the soil is really hard and dry. But it's summer. Some kid on vacation probably picked up the rocks on the path and threw them blindly, not knowing a cottage was nearby. It could have been a couple of kids. Maybe they dared each other."

"That sounds plausible," Shannon murmured, wondering how far a kid could throw a rock. Her cottage was a fair distance from the path. She wasn't sure she could throw a rock that far, much less a child. But a grown man could.

"You don't sound very convinced," Luke said. His face hovered over hers, his eyes dark with concern. "Has something like this happened before?"

Shannon hesitated, tempted to mention the phone call she'd had last night. But there had been nothing threatening about that call. He'd interpret it as a wrong number and think she was a nutcase, making a mountain out of a molehill. The last thing she wanted to do was give him an excuse to leave her employ.

"N-no, of course not," she said, breaking eye contact with him. With trembling fingers she removed the pink sunhat from her daughter's head and smoothed Samantha's silky hair. She felt Luke standing there, waiting, felt the strength of his fingers cupping her bare shoulder and the heat of his body radiating toward her. Without daring to look, she knew she'd see compassion and understanding in his eyes. The desire to unburden herself rose within her, pulsing against her ribs like a second heartbeat, but the enormity of what was at stake—her future and her daughter's future—gave her the strength to resist. No one must know who she really was, what she'd done.

She took a step back, forcing him to release her. His hand dropped from her shoulder and curled into a tight fist against his thigh as if he realized he'd overstepped his bounds.

Shannon decided the best way to deal with the situation and the disconcerting sparkling sensation on her shoulder where he had touched her was to ignore it. She sucked in a shallow breath and dredged up a smile. "Samantha and I usually eat lunch early. You're welcome to join us. I'm sure you haven't had time to buy groceries. I've got some leftover quiche I was going to heat up."

"Thanks. I'll take you up on your offer today, but I don't want to be an imposition."

She met his gaze over the top of Samantha's head. There was something precarious about the way she was feeling right now. The intensity in Luke's eyes seemed to weaken her bones and interfere with her ability to fill her lungs with oxygen. "Don't be too grateful for the invitation," she said breathlessly. "Samantha has less than perfect table manners. She wears most of her food."

His slow easy grin ignited a fireball of warmth in the pit of her belly. "Sounds entertaining."

Shannon nodded, irrationally pleased he'd accepted her invitation. The weather was fine enough to eat outdoors, but the thought of being in the open after the rock-throwing incident made her nervous, so she set two places at the counter in the kitchen, using place mats she'd sewn herself in anticipation of having a normal life. Not that she'd invited anyone to join her for a meal since she'd arrived in Blossom Valley. Because Luke was her first guest and she didn't want him to know how frightened she was, she gathered her courage and stepped outside long enough to snip a small bouquet of petunias and alyssum to decorate the table. Spying the rock near the planter, she picked it up. Checking to make sure no one was near the lake's shore, she threw it toward the water. It went farther than she thought, landing in the water with a splash. She gave the second rock the same treatment. Any kid who played Little League could probably equal or better her efforts. Maybe Luke was right and it had been kids messing around.

Bolstered by this thought, Shannon let herself enjoy the simple pleasure of sharing a meal with another adult.

Not that Samantha made it easy. Her daughter's

hands were everywhere—smearing her puréed meal of veal, carrots and bananas on her highchair tray, her bib and in her hair. Shannon gave a yelp of surprise as her daughter grabbed the baby spoon and flung a glob of purée across the counter and onto Luke's T-shirt. Samantha chortled with delight, proud of her accomplishment.

"Good aim, kid," he told Samantha with a wink as he wiped at the spot with his napkin.

"You see, I wasn't exaggerating," Shannon exclaimed, attempting to snatch back the spoon before Samantha used it as a catapult again.

"No, you weren't, but with all my nieces and nephews, I'm used to dining off my clothes. You don't exactly seem shocked by your daughter's outrageous table manners. I'll bet you have several siblings and a half-dozen nieces and nephews."

"Actually, I'm an only child," Shannon replied without thinking, distracted by the tug-of-war she was having with Samantha over the spoon. "Rob's older brother has stepkids, but he lives in Texas—I only met them a couple of times." Realizing her inadvertent slip, Shannon clamped her mouth shut before she revealed anything more personal than that.

Talking to Luke was too darn easy.

As if she wasn't already distracted by Samantha's antics with her food, Luke distracted her in a way that made her feel off-kilter. She didn't know why she should be so entranced by the little details of his strong face, but she was. He had a tiny scar just above the right corner of his mouth, nicely proportioned ears that made her fingers tingle to trace their shape, and more corded muscles in the column of his throat than should be allowed by law.

Shannon traded Samantha a digestive biscuit for the spoon. While her daughter gnawed on the cookie, Shannon sampled the salad and the wedge of broccoli quiche on her own plate and dwelled on the fact that, in addition to appreciating Luke's hard-as-steel good looks, she liked how he responded to Samantha. She had a feeling that Rob, who'd always been meticulous in his appearance and wanted their home to be the epitome of organization and cleanliness, wouldn't have taken this stage of Samantha's life so easily in stride. Rob had owned his own events-planning firm and he'd hated to have any deviations, major or minor, to his plans. And babies were major deviations, tantamount to discovering that the printer had screwed up the order for the conference packets and the workshops would have to proceed without the necessary accompanying materials.

By the time Shannon finished her lunch, Samantha was yawning in her high chair, her dark eyelashes fluttering as her eyes fought a losing battle to remain open. Cookie stuck to her lips as her chin drooped to her chest, coming to rest in a sticky blob of mashed banana clinging to the bib she wore. Shannon couldn't help thinking with maternal pride that her daughter was absolutely, beautifully perfect just the way she was. "Someone's ready for her nap."

"You go put her to bed—I'll clean up," Luke offered, reaching for her plate.

Shannon wasn't about to argue with anyone who was as easy on female eyes as Luke was and did the dishes. But she sternly reminded herself as she detached Samantha from her high chair and lifted her daughter's warm sticky body into her arms that she was in no position to think of Luke as anything but her temporary employee.

It took a good fifteen minutes to get Samantha cleaned up, changed and tucked into her crib. When Shannon emerged from her daughter's bedroom, the dishes were washed and put away in the cupboard, and the counter and high chair had been thoroughly wiped. But there was no sign of Luke. The faint distant whine of the miter saw told her that he'd returned to the garage to finish cutting the letter boxes.

Shannon was tempted to go check on his progress, but the urge felt more like an attempt to seek out his company than inspect his work. The pieces would be just as she wanted them. And she had work to do, signs to paint. With a sigh, she sat down at the table and reached for a small plastic bottle of apple-green acrylic paint. After squeezing a puddle of paint onto a palette, she selected a fan-shaped brush from a jar and started work on the evergreens that were part of the design of her welcome signs. She didn't need a friend or companionship or even a man to make her happy. She'd already achieved her own happiness. All she needed to maintain it was Samantha and a place to earn a living in peace.

LUKE COULDN'T GET OUT of Mary's house soon enough with the glass that she'd drunk from at lunch concealed in a plastic bag. He stopped at the sandbox to search for the rocks that had been thrown at Mary and Samantha, hoping one of them might harbor a latent fingerprint, but they'd disappeared. Mary must have gotten rid of them when she'd gone outside earlier. He should have gotten to them first.

Cursing his carelessness, Luke hurried out to the garage and hid the glass in the scrap-wood box— maybe the fingerprints on it would give him another piece of the puzzle to Mary's life. While Mary had been putting Samantha down for her nap, he'd taken advantage of the opportunity to check the medicine cabinet in the bathroom for prescription medications that would have a name typed on the label. But there weren't any.

Her fingerprints on the glass might confirm her identity once and for all. And maybe give him a hint as to what she was running from. At least he knew now that her husband's name was Rob. Detective Vaughn ought to be able to find out if a Rob Calder had died in the months prior to Mary's appearance in Blossom Valley. A death record would help substantiate her identity, give them a city of residence.

He'd take the glass over to the RCMP detachment as soon as he finished his shift.

Luke slipped on a pair of safety goggles and a dust mask. While his mind mulled over theories about Mary's identity and her real story, he methodically measured, cut and sanded the pine pieces for the letter boxes.

Hours slipped away. Mary didn't come out to the garage. When Luke had finished, he brushed the sawdust off his clothes, carefully stacked the assembled letter boxes and carried them to her cottage.

"Finished already?" she asked, coming to open the screen door for him. Luke noticed she'd locked it. Samantha was awake from her nap and happily emptying plastic containers from a kitchen drawer. Luke set the stack of pieces on Mary's worktable. The welcome signs she'd been working on were completed, various designs of trees, flowers and vegetables painted on each.

"Hey, these are excellent." The whimsical renderings were not quite what one would expect from someone involved in a murder.

"Thanks," she said softly, blushing. The pale peach color spilled over her tanned cheeks. "A couple coats of polyurethane and they'll be weatherproof."

Maybe it was the fact that he'd searched her home and stolen the glass from her table that hindered his ability to meet her gaze. Maybe it had something to do with his growing awareness that despite his purpose for being here, he was undeniably attracted to her. Even while the tight knot in his stomach told him how unforgivable those feelings were, a part of him responded to the melodious sound of her voice and the sunny appeal of her smile. Which was all the more reason for him to do what he'd come here to do and get the hell out of here.

He gave her a piece of paper with the new phone number at his cottage written on it. Even though he worried she'd feel he was intruding on her space, he told her to feel free to call him if she got worried or heard strange bumps in the night. "I'm just a few minutes away on foot."

"We'll be fine, but I appreciate having your number, anyway." Her voice was firm, but he noticed how she caught her lower lip between her teeth as she stuck the phone number to the refrigerator door with a magnet.

He placed the key to the garage on her worktable, not wanting to risk even the slightest accidental touch of their hands. "The workshop is locked up tight. I'll see you tomorrow."

Luke quickly headed to his cottage to shower and change, Mary's drinking glass safely in his possession. An hour later, he was pulling into the parking lot of the RCMP detachment, a nondescript building with a yellow brick facade. Luke showed his badge to the detachment commander, Staff Sergeant Todd Rayford, a tall gaunt man with a jaw like an icebreaker and hooded eyes, and explained he was working on a murder investigation. Rayford summoned someone in the Ident Section to lift the prints off the glass. Then the prints were faxed to Ottawa to see if a record could be found.

Luke waited impatiently for Detective Vaughn to call him with the results, passing the time in conversation with Rayford. He tried not to think what would happen if there was a record of Mary's prints and possibly an outstanding arrest warrant.

It shouldn't matter to him that if Mary was arrested, Samantha would be taken away from her and put under the care of child services. What mattered was what this woman might be able to tell them about his wife's murder.

When his cell phone rang thirty minutes after the fax was sent, Luke felt the tight knot in his stomach harden to stone.

Would he finally get some answers?

Chapter Four

"Sorry, Calder, Ottawa says there's no record of the prints," Detective Vaughn said without preamble.

Luke swore under his breath in frustration and paced the length of the interview room the detachment commander had allowed him to use for privacy. So much for hoping for easy answers. Whoever the woman was masquerading under his wife's name, she didn't have a criminal record.

Luke was uncertain whether this was good news or bad.

He jabbed his fingers through his hair. "I've got a first name for you on the husband. It's Rob, presumably Calder. Getting personal data out of her is like boring a hole through granite with a toothpick."

Vaughn laughed, a raspy sound that grated on Luke's ears. "That easy, huh? No one ever said detective work was a walk in the park. Just be patient and keep drilling, Calder, until you get something solid. I'll check out the husband's name and get back to you."

As a cop Luke knew the best detective work was the result of hours and hours of dogged determination and unfailing attention to the tiniest detail. One seemingly insignificant piece of information could be the clue that would break a case wide open. He just had to keep feeding Vaughn whatever information he could lay his hands on and hope something would turn into a significant lead.

He climbed back into his rental car and drove to the local newspaper office, hoping the archives might provide him with some straightforward answers. Mary had told him Samantha was almost ten months old. Was it possible she'd placed an announcement in the paper after her daughter's birth?

At the newspaper office, Luke asked to see back issues of the *Weekly Gazette* dated a month before and several months after Samantha's birth. But after an hour ensconced in an uncomfortable wooden chair scanning page after page of newsprint, all he had to show for his efforts was a crick in his neck. There was no birth announcement proclaiming the proud parents and grandparents.

He'd have to keep on being patient for as long as it took.

SHANNON PUSHED Samantha's stroller along the path that twined through the Shady Pines Resort in a blatant act of taking back what she felt was hers—the right to enjoy her life without fear. Ever since Luke had left her cottage this afternoon, she'd felt her sense of security lessening. Her ears pricked at every slight sound, her sense of isolation growing until her cottage felt more like a prison than a house of hard-won freedom.

She'd never been so angry with herself. She'd hired Luke to help with her business, and while she couldn't find fault with his character or the quality of his work, she realized to her dismay that she'd nearly lost something precious in the bargain. One day in a man's presence and she was reverting back to the spineless woman she'd once been. She could justify turning to Luke for help this morning when she and Samantha had nearly been hit by those rocks because he happened to be nearby. Had he not been there to go after the culprit, she would have called Bill Oakes to handle the problem.

What she couldn't justify was the weakness inside her that acknowledged that having a man like Luke on the premises made her feel safer. She couldn't fault Luke for his well-intentioned and noble offer to call him if she heard any strange noises in the night. But she could fault herself for being tempted to use him as a crutch. She had no one to blame but herself for allowing the insidious thought to sneak into her head that she couldn't handle things on her own.

Shannon's fingers tightened on the stroller's handle. She didn't need a man to protect her. She was smart enough and capable enough to protect herself and her daughter.

Her worst enemy was not Rob. It was fear.

And Shannon was determined to conquer it here and now. Shady Pines was her home. She knew every curve in the path, every tree, every blade of grass. On any other balmy evening like tonight where the sun hung like a huge rosy grapefruit on the horizon, ready to be plucked by nightfall's hand, she'd be out taking a walk with Samantha. Breathing in the fresh air, listening to the chorus of crickets, exchanging pleasantries with her neighbors and the summer guests. Tonight was not going to be any different.

She wouldn't even let herself look through the trees at Abner's decrepit cottage as she passed. She didn't want to know if Luke was home in the midst of cooking his dinner or sitting on the step reading the paper or dreaming about owning his own business. She would respect his privacy as much as she wanted him to respect hers.

Swimmers frolicked in the water around the floating dock as Shannon pushed the stroller down to the beach, parking it in the thick sand. She waved a greeting at Alice Nesbitt and a half dozen of the elderly woman's grandchildren, who were swarming an ice-cream cart. Force of habit had her seeking out all the faces on the crescent-shaped beach, sorting the unfamiliar from the familiar, her heart racing with anxiety until each and every person was identified. She'd seen the family staying in the cottage next door several times this week. Her eyes narrowed on the person manning the ice-cream cart. It was a teenage boy, not a man as she'd thought at first glance. It took her a moment to place him. Ah, yes. He was Donna White's son. Donna was a fellow crafter who sold her work to many of the same vendors as Shannon. Though Shannon couldn't recall the young man's name, she remembered meeting him a couple of months ago at Glorie's Gifts Galore. He'd been helping his mom deliver stock.

Certain all was as it should be, Shannon kicked off

her shoes and socks, then bent over to remove Samantha's sandals before lifting her daughter from the stroller. ''Come on, baby, let's get our toes wet.''

The water lapping at their feet felt pleasantly lukewarm. Samantha squealed with delight with every timid step, holding tight to Shannon's leg. Her daughter's delight at this simplest of pleasures was contagious. A sense of peace, tranquil as the evening air, settled around Shannon as she gazed out at Kettle Lake's misty-blue border.

''Good evening.''

Shannon whirled around at the sound of Luke's voice. Whatever peace and confidence she'd found by forcing herself outside into the world beyond her cottage was shaken by the sight of him in royal-blue nylon swimming trunks and a black tank top that clung like a second skin to his chest, leaving nothing of his physique to the imagination. And the last thing she wanted was images of Luke to infiltrate her imagination more than they already had. Her gaze dropped from the tuffs of dark hair matting his chest to his bronzed legs as if somehow she could prevent her mind from cataloging the powerful combination of sinew, muscle and bone. Or the dark coarse hair that was all male and very, very sexy. He was carrying a beige beach towel in one hand, which made her think he'd come to the beach for a swim.

''Hi.'' Her voice came out sharper than she intended, almost angry. One look at him, and the urges and desires she'd told herself she was not going to yield to were already swirling in the pit of her stomach, threatening mutiny. *I do not need a man for protection,* she reminded herself sternly.

What about to love? Companionship? Sex? More babies? a subversive voice demanded from a deep corner of her mind. Her gaze darted to Luke's face. His eyes were the same gray-blue as the water and filled with concern.

"You okay?" he asked, tossing the beach towel onto the sand a few feet from them. "You look a bit pale."

Shannon's irritation grew. A rational part of her knew that he was only inquiring to be nice. Still, she resented the underlying implication that because her truck happened to get a flat tire the other day and she'd been on the receiving end of some kid's throw this morning, she might be somehow transmitting the idea that she wasn't capable of handling these incidents. She took a deep breath and forced a smile. "I'm great. Nothing perilous has befallen me or Samantha since this morning. Are you getting settled in?"

"Yes. The fridge is full of groceries—" He broke off as Samantha toddled across the few feet between them, her tiny fingers grasping the hair on his legs. "Come to say hi, Sammy girl?" He loosened Samantha's fingers, then tucked his hands beneath the toddler's arm and lifted her slightly, swinging her so that her bare feet skimmed the surface of the water. Samantha kicked her feet, splashing both adults.

The combined sounds of her daughter's squeals and Luke's laughter touched a nerve. Shannon tucked a stray strand of blond hair behind her ears and tamped down an irrational urge to stop him from interacting with her daughter. It seemed selfish and petty when Luke looked as if he was enjoying himself as much as Samantha.

But seeing the two of them together made her realize that the very act of protecting Samantha from her father was depriving her of a world of things that little girls do with their daddies.

"Maybe you shouldn't do that—swing her, I mean," she finished lamely. "She just ate."

Luke didn't question her. But those gray-blue eyes seemed to guess too much as he gently planted Samantha feetfirst into the water in front of Shannon. "Sorry, I should have asked."

"N-no, it's okay." Shannon felt a tightness in her chest and the burn of tears in her eyes. She was being bitchy about nothing. She put a hand out, touching his arm, wanting to explain. But the hard hot feel of his skin threw her thoughts into further disarray. Made her feel more off balance. "It's just you made me think of her dad for a moment, and I…" Her voice trailed off. Her eyes searched his face, hoping he'd somehow understand what she couldn't articulate.

A corner of his mouth lifted in a smile that was gentle and nonjudgmental. "Don't worry about it, no offense taken," he said, trapping her fingers against his arm for a brief instant. Then he stepped back, and Shannon felt a twinge of loss at the break of contact with his body. He pulled the tank top over his shoulders and tossed it onto the sand beside his towel, granting her an unrestricted view of the thick matt of hair that covered his chest and arrowed down into the waistband of his swimming trunks. He flexed his shoulders. "I'm going for a swim. Care to join me?"

Shannon swallowed hard. *Sexual attraction.* That was the only name she dared give what was going on between her and Luke. What woman wouldn't be affected by a man who looked as tantalizingly male as Luke did in a bathing suit? Shannon would bet Alice Nesbitt, who frequently indulged in those thick spicy novels with bare-chested men on the covers, was having heart palpitations. "We don't have our suits with us. Besides, it's just about Samantha's bedtime. But thanks for the offer."

Luke's eyes locked on hers, something in them pulling at her on another level. "Maybe another time?" he suggested in a low tone that seemed only for her ears.

"I don't swim." It was a lie, but Shannon figured one more lie wouldn't matter on top of all the others she'd told since she'd assumed Mary Calder's identity. And she didn't want to encourage anything personal between her and Luke. "But you enjoy yourself. I'll see you tomorrow."

Samantha protested at being lifted out of the water, but Shannon turned a deaf ear as she carried her back to the stroller.

Alice Nesbitt called out to her as she passed. Shannon reluctantly stopped. "Just wanted you to know, Mary," Alice said, peeling back the wrapper on an ice-cream sandwich, "that Bill went round to all the cottages this afternoon. You won't have to worry about anyone doing anything so reckless again. I personally think it must have been Roger's older boy,

Adam, since they're in the cottage nearest yours. But Roger insists the kids were with him the whole time." Alice sniffed. "Roger is a lawyer. He makes piles of money, but I never trust what lawyers say. His mother—my sister Peggy—was very good at bending the truth to suit herself. Still, Bill had a stern talk with Roger's children, anyway."

The relations between the Oakes' vast family were an endless source of wonder to Shannon. Being an only child, she always thought she'd be so grateful to have a brother or sister she couldn't possibly find fault with them. But Alice heaped both praise and criticism on her siblings and their offspring in equal measure. "Thanks, Alice. I'll have to thank Bill next time I see him."

"Anytime. We're mostly family here. We look after our own. There's one other thing, Mary…"

Shannon sensed the older woman's hesitation. "Yes?"

"When Bill and I were talking about how seriously either of you could have been hurt, he realized that he didn't have an emergency contact for you on record."

"He doesn't?" Shannon frowned, pretending it was an oversight rather than a deliberate omission on her part. She'd never gotten back to Bill about the emergency contact and he'd forgotten about it—until now. Alice's eyes were too discerning. "I'll have to get him the information right away." She jiggled Samantha on her hip, who was squirming, trying to get down. "Now if you'll excuse me, I really have to go. Samantha's reached her limit for one evening."

"Of course, dear."

Shannon plodded across the sandy beach, trying to distract Samantha from wanting to go back in the water with promises of a bath. Now what was she going to do? She'd traded the problem she'd hoped to conquer by venturing out this evening for another more pressing one. How could she give Bill Oakes her mother's name or her aunt's, much less their phone number and address? Any connection between this life and her old one could put her daughter at risk. But Shannon had a feeling that Alice and Bill would insist she give them something tangible. A faint breeze stirred the hair on the back of her neck as she deposited Samantha in her stroller. Shannon glanced out at the lake where she could see Luke gliding smoothly through the water and felt a frisson of uncertainty blow over her body. So many lies.

What had happened to the Shannon Mulligan she'd once been, the woman who'd played by the rules, who'd reported the incidents of her ex-husband's abuse and naively believed the law would protect her?

She'd had her blinders ripped off.

Now the only law she still held sacred was protecting Samantha at all costs.

LUKE FELT MORE like a voyeur than a cop, watching her.

Maybe he was being paranoid, but Mary had seemed in an awful hurry to leave the beach once he'd arrived. He wasn't sure whether his playing with Sammy had tapped into a vein of grief as Mary had suggested, or whether it was a feeble excuse she hoped he'd believe. Mary acted like a woman on the run.

Maybe the instincts she'd developed were subconsciously warning her not to trust him, and she was listening to them.

All the more reason for Luke to take things slow and easy. Luke waited until Mary was wheeling Samantha back onto the path before coming in from the water and reaching for his towel. The ice-cream vendor gave him a probing look as if silently inquiring whether Luke wanted to finish off the evening with an ice-cream bar. "No thanks," Luke replied with a grin, realizing the vendor was the same sullen-faced kid he'd seen on the resort grounds earlier this morning. Only now he was literally glowering at Luke over his refusal to buy something.

Luke pulled on his shirt and draped the towel around his neck. He'd spend what was left of the daylight familiarizing himself with the resort's grounds in the area surrounding Mary's cottage. As he'd quickly assessed the other morning when he'd conducted his initial surveillance of her residence, there were countless places one could conduct surveillance from: the water, the shoreline and the clumps of trees and vegetation that granted each site privacy. No one would think twice about spotting someone in the bush or in a boat with a pair of binoculars around his or her neck.

Luke didn't like the thought of Mary and Samantha being so vulnerable. At least Mary seemed to have a good head on her shoulders, and she was cautious.

Nightfall finally chased Luke back into his own cottage. But he was up early the next morning, jogging along the resort's paths, keeping an eye out for anything unusual.

Still, he felt a measure of relief when he arrived at Mary's cottage just before eleven and heard her melodious voice drifting through the screen door. She was obviously on the phone. Luke could hear Samantha banging something together in the background—pots and pans?

"I'm glad you called, Bill," Mary was saying. "I've got that emergency contact number you wanted. I'm sorry I forgot to give it to you earlier."

Luke stilled, willing his body not to make a sound that might betray his presence. Emergency contact number? He concentrated on memorizing the phone number that Mary read off for a Norah Kent, his ears straining to hear each number in the din Samantha was making. He didn't recognize the area code. "That's my mom's number in Moncton, New Brunswick. She and my aunt Jayne live together now," Mary explained. "Do you need an address, too?"

A brief silence was punctuated by the metallic clatter of something hitting the floor. Luke silently prayed that Bill would insist on an address.

Mary's voice rose. "No? Great, well, I won't keep you..."

Realizing the call was about to come to an end, Luke silently backed off the front stoop and retraced his steps down the path.

Maybe, just maybe, he'd heard enough.

SHANNON'S CHIN SANK to her chest in silent gratitude as she hung up the phone. She'd done it. Bill hadn't questioned her or asked for an address, though she'd been prepared to give him the address that went along with the phone number she'd culled from an advertisement in a crafts magazine. And she'd used her mother and aunt's maiden name. For a moment she let the adrenaline rush of that little success boost her confidence. One day at a time. She would continue to win one day at a time.

She patted the advertisement in the magazine lying open on her kitchen counter. What more could she want out of life?

The answer seemed to manifest itself in the flash of movement in the yard. Shannon turned her head and saw Luke through the screen door. What on earth was he doing? Walking backward? Doing the Mambo?

Shannon gave Samantha a quick glance to be sure her daughter was happy with her pots and plastic containers before moving to the screen door. Luke noticed her as soon as she appeared in the doorway and made a quick light movement that resembled a two-step.

"Little early for dancing, isn't it?" she asked, amused, unhooking the latch. "My, my, you're a man of many hidden talents."

Luke looked engagingly embarrassed at being caught. He shrugged and took two fluid steps forward, his eyes locking on to hers. "Some people dance by moonlight or candlelight. I prefer sunlight. Of course, a few beers help," he added teasingly, the rhythmic sway of his hips awakening an answering response in her. His eyes narrowed on her and his voice tinged with unmistakable huskiness, asked, "Do you dance, Mary?"

"Are you asking me to dance with you?" Shannon asked in disbelief, grateful for the screen door that separated them. Her fingers clung to the handle, holding the door closed.

Luke took a step closer. She could feel the magnetism of his pull, egging her on to join him on the stepping stones for a silly harmless dance. "Why do you sound so shocked?"

The sensuality in his voice rippled over her, warming her as she imagined the morning sun would warm her if she dared to step outside with him…as she knew the touch of his fingers would warm her if she let him take her in his arms.

Her fingers grew slippery on the door handle. "You do realize there's no music, don't you?"

He paused and spread his arms wide. "Ah, Mary, there's music—a whole orchestra. Listen."

Shannon stared at him and listened, hearing the inviting song of the birds. He was right. It was beautiful. Her heart fluttered against her ribs, baited by the temptation he offered. She battled the urge to push the door open and join him. "None of your references told me you were this crazy."

"You probably didn't ask." He took another step forward and held his hand out to her. "Come on, join me. I haven't danced in ages." His voice caught, and Shannon found herself wondering whom he'd last danced with, and when.

"I can't leave Samantha," she protested, searching for an excuse to end this lunacy.

"Bring her with you." Luke stepped onto the porch. "There's room on the dance floor."

Shannon had to concentrate hard not to greedily absorb the rugged contours of his body, the sexy shadow coating his jaw. Her mouth gaped open. "I shouldn't. I'm your employer."

"Chicken."

She knew he was only teasing, but still, he'd unknowingly touched a nerve. She was not now and would never be a coward. "Me, chicken?"

He was so close Shannon could see his chest rise and fall and the veins standing out along his sculpted arms. "Yes, you," he said, adamant. His lips curved into a knowing smile. "Next you'll claim you don't dance."

Shannon fixed him with a belligerent gaze even as a second rush of adrenaline made her feel inexplicably giddy. "I don't."

His brows lifted. "I'll teach you. Join me before the song finishes."

She was about to argue that the song could go on for hours, but realized he'd only come up with another reason something precious would be irrevocably gone if they missed this opportunity to dance together in the sunlight. A part of her acknowledged swiftly, urgently, that Luke was right. Life was the here and now. Tomorrow, next week or next year, all she'd worked to achieve might be lost. How many opportunities would she have to dance in the sunlight with a handsome man?

Maybe not more than once in a lifetime. There was no room in her life for someone like Luke. But she had time for just one dance.

"All right. Hold your horses." Shannon plucked Samantha from her nest of saucepans and spoons and carried her to the door, her heart rising in her throat at the sight of Luke waiting for them, standing taller than a bridegroom in worn jeans and a black T-shirt. His eyes had lost the teasing glint she'd glimpsed moments ago and were now dark with potent intent.

For a moment she felt her courage receding, slipping down inside her with the breath that couldn't seem to escape from her lungs. But she'd promised herself she'd never let a man intimidate her again, so she pushed the screen door open with her daughter in her arms. What could be the harm of just one dance?

LUKE DIDN'T KNOW how nearly getting caught eavesdropping had turned into an impromptu dance in the sunlight, but he was fiercely glad it was happening.

It should be silly, ridiculous even, except he felt anything but ridiculous as Mary's fingers lightly settled on his palm. He felt wildly, thoroughly alive. Pretty had been the wrong word to describe her. Sensational was better. She belonged out here in the sunshine, the golden light bathing her cheeks, illuminating her hair, caressing her slim figure. She wore a short flowered sundress today with those skinny straps that seemed to dare him to push them off her shoulders, taste the satin skin beneath.

Her lips curved into a smile that was sheer bravado. "Lost your nerve?"

"Never." His fingers tightened around hers proprietarily. He had two names and a phone number. A means of positively identifying Mary. And then what? he asked himself as he gazed down into her eyes. He honestly didn't know. He'd deal with that when the time came. "Shh!" he admonished her. "I'm listening to the beat of the music.'' With a slight tug on her wrist, he drew her and Samantha into his arms, leading them into a waltz.

Mary laughed, the sound bubbling out of her, spilling around them until Luke couldn't hear the melody of the birds. But her laughter was musical enough, so he danced to that, Samantha squashed cozily between their bodies, her eyes wide and her fingers gripping Luke's T-shirt as they twirled over the grass and the stepping stones.

''Where on earth did you learn to dance like this?'' Mary asked breathlessly, keeping pace with him.

She felt light as gossamer in his arms, as if the first breath of desert wind would whisk her away. Luke splayed his fingers over the small of her back, anchoring mother and child to him. ''My dad. Family weddings.'' *His own wedding.* Actually his dad had made sure that both his sons could dance properly with their brides. Luke expected to feel the biting loss at the memory of his first dance with his bride, but all he felt was the serendipitous joy of this moment, with *this* Mary.

Mary's eyes were impossible to read, reflecting conflicting images of pleasure and uncertainty. But that didn't stop him from wanting to know every thought that went on in that creative mind of hers. She tilted her head back, her pink lips moist and parted. An unquenchable desire to finish the dance with a kiss raced full-throttle through Luke's blood.

''Tell me the truth,'' she said, a flirtatious edge to her voice. ''Why did you want me to dance with you?''

"The truth?" Luke wondered fleetingly what the truth was. To cover the fact that he'd been eavesdropping on her conversation? Or was it because finding her safe and unharmed in her cottage this morning made him feel inexplicably happy and more alive than he'd felt in a long time? The answer that came to his lips surprised him with its simple truth. "Because I haven't felt like dancing in a long time, and suddenly the urge was there. I felt if I didn't dance, it would go away and never come back."

"I haven't danced in a long time, either," she admitted. "Not since my wedding night."

Luke was intrigued by this admission. Maybe she hadn't been lying when she'd told him her husband was dead. She sounded as if she, too, was mourning her spouse. "Is it painful now—to dance, I mean?"

"No, you haven't stepped on my toes once." Her teasing smile nearly sent Luke right over the edge of coherent thought as his body fixated on the notion of kissing her. Instinctively he lowered his head, breathing in the jasmine scent of her hair, his lips hungry for the taste of her mouth. "Why'd you agree to dance with me?" he demanded, struggling to regain some control.

Her laughter speared him, tortured him with its ebullient sweetness. She was enjoying this as much as he was. "Because you dared me."

"I thought so."

Luke stopped dancing. The birds continued their infectious tune, but he could only hear the blood pounding in his ears. He was vaguely aware of Samantha curiously watching him and her mother. "Mary," he breathed, giving in to the desire to kiss her. Here. Now.

Shannon was certain that Luke intended to kiss her. She could see the debate taking place in his eyes. Felt her heart shrivel as he called her by a name that wasn't hers. She yanked her fingers from the luring trap of his hand and placed them over his mouth, stopping the kiss.

This was wrong. Terribly wrong.

"Please don't! I like you, and I admit there's some chemistry between us, but we don't know anything about each other." The heat of his lips was so distracting against her palm she tripped over her words. "And even if we did know each other better, I'm not ready for this. Not now anyway…" *Maybe not ever,* she amended silently, biting hard on her lower lip.

"What happened to your husband, Mary?"

Shannon blinked, taken aback by his abrupt question. "What do you mean?"

"You're obviously hurting about something. Maybe it would help if you talked about it." He gripped her upper arms. His touch, though restraining, was infinitely gentle, inviting her to let him share in her troubles.

She jerked backward, relieved that he released her instantly. Samantha let out a small whimper as Luke's shirt was ripped from her fingers. Shannon's body knotted with tension as she forced a light tone into her voice. "Thanks for the offer, but talking only reminds me of things that are too painful to think about."

"If you change your mind, I'm a good listener." He lifted a hand as if to touch her again.

Not for the kind of story she had to tell. Shannon felt her body tremble as if conspiring to lean into his touch against her consent. She averted her gaze, dropping a kiss on Samantha's dark hair to hide the tiny flutter of disappointment as his hand fell to his side.

Nothing could happen between them. Not as long as she was Mary Calder. She forced her thoughts to her present needs—a lover was definitely not among them. "Wait here. I'll get the key to the workshop. I want you to work on some different patterns today." Shannon hurried into the cottage as fast as her wobbly legs would carry her. No matter how sexy and understanding Luke was, she wasn't about to drag him into the fraud that was her life.

HE WATCHED HER DANCE with her husband through the lenses of the binoculars. The little slut. Laughing with him, teasing him, withholding kisses. How touching. Mary Calder became more and more interesting with each passing day. She thought she was oh, so clever, disappearing like that, but it seemed the slut had more secrets. He wondered how her husband would react when he found out she was cheating on him. He'd seen them sniffing around her cottage in the dead of night. With the child's dark hair and eyes, it wouldn't be long before Calder figured out the brat wasn't his.

Calder would be mad enough to kill. Which gave him the most interesting idea of getting rid of Mary once and for all....

Chapter Five

Shannon stayed up until after midnight, working and trying to keep herself from thinking about how a man like Luke would kiss a woman. Slowly. Thoroughly. Sensuously. And yes, teasingly. Shannon frowned at the snippets of silk ivy, dried flowers, ribbons, mushroom birds and Spanish moss littering her worktable as her breasts tingled with an aching fullness. She'd had an incredibly productive evening assembling the picket-fence decorations Luke had cut for her today. Glorie's order was ready for delivery, though Shannon would have to get up early to apply the last coat of finish to the letter boxes. Hiring a woodworker was proving to be a sound decision.

She just shouldn't have hired Luke.

He was too handsome, too easy to talk to, and too sensitive to her moods. Just too distracting for her peace of mind. She'd already lost her head and her heart over one man; she wasn't about to behave so recklessly again. Still, heat spiraled inside her as she collected stray coils of Spanish moss into a plastic bag, remembering her foolhardy impetuousness and then being twirled around her front yard in Luke's arms.

The naked hunger in his eyes when he'd leaned down to kiss her.

Thank God she'd been able to gather her wits in time and prevent that mistake from happening.

Shannon dropped the plastic bag onto the table and stretched the stiffness from her shoulders. When she was in town tomorrow, she'd check her post-office box. Her ad for a woodworker had appeared in yesterday's edition of the paper.

Hiring a permanent replacement for Luke would be the most sensible way of severing the attraction growing between them without offending Luke by firing him.

Shannon hit the light switch. Darkness flooded the room, drowning her. A noise reached her ears over the nightly refrain of insects. Was that Samantha? She froze, listening. No, it had sounded more like a snapping branch somewhere outside. Shannon moved silently through the darkened room to the nearest window, lifting the lace panel to peer out into the night. A scattering of stars dotted the sky but did little to illuminate the trees and shrubbery concealed by night's dark blanket.

Shannon heard a distinct rustling. Of leaves? Someone or something moving through the brush? A shadowy form slipped between the cottage and her garage and crossed her lawn. Unmistakably human—though she couldn't tell if it was male or female. Whichever, the figure was definitely moving away from her cottage.

Fear raked Shannon's spine. Was it someone out for a midnight walk on the grounds? Across her front lawn, though? Options flew through her terrified mind, options that included the possibility that Rob was stalking her again. The doors and windows were securely bolted. She could call Bill…or Luke. Certainly not the police.

The figure disappeared somewhere down her drive. Shannon stared into the night until her eyes ached, waiting for the person to return. Fifteen minutes passed before it occurred to her that it might have been Bill or Luke checking on her before they retired for the night.

Shannon felt the tendrils of fear loosen their grip on her heart, though she was still as jumpy as a child on a sugar high. Moving through the cottage, she double-checked the locks on her doors and windows. They were all secure. Samantha slept like an angel in the crib wedged in the tiny bedroom next to Shannon's.

Senses still on alert for the slightest hint of danger, Shannon brushed her teeth in the dark, washed her face and pulled on a short summer nightgown. Then she gathered her pillow and a sheet from the bed and made herself comfortable in the rocking chair, which she drew up within arm's reach of the phone in the kitchen.

Beneath the folds of the sheet she concealed a hammer. Anyone attempting to enter her cottage in the middle of the night would get a welcome they'd never forget.

"I'M SORRY, there's no one here by that name."

"Are you sure?" Luke demanded, tension throbbing in his temple. He repeated the number back to the woman.

"That's the right number, but there's no one by the name of Kent working here. Never has been, as I recall."

"Working here?" Luke echoed. "I was under the impression I was calling a residence."

"This is a floral shop in Moncton, New Brunswick."

Had he misheard the number? Luke swallowed hard. "I'm sorry to disturb you, but it's really important that I reach Jayne and Norah Kent. It's a family emergency. Maybe I got the number wrong. Would you be able to check it for me in your local phone book?"

The woman sighed. "Sure. Kent's the last name, you say?"

"Yes."

"It doesn't ring any bells, but I'll check." Luke held his breath as the woman flipped through the pages of the phone book, muttering surnames as she went. "I'm sorry, there are no Kent listings at all."

Luke thanked the woman and hung up. Now what? Mary had said her mother and aunt had just moved, so maybe they weren't listed in the phone book yet. But the long-distance-information operator informed him there were no listings published or unpublished for Jayne and Norah Kent in Moncton. Either Luke had misheard the number or Mary had given Bill the wrong number. And the possibility that she might have done so deliberately made Luke want to kick something.

He punched in Detective Vaughn's number. Maybe Vaughn could find out something about Jayne and Norah Kent. If they even existed.

"I DON'T NEED a protector."

Luke was taken aback by Mary's abrupt greeting and her appearance when he tapped on the frame of the screen door Friday morning at ten-thirty. Her blond hair was mussed as if she'd just lifted her head from the pillow. The purple smudges under her eyes suggested that she hadn't spent much of the night in restful slumber. She gave him a baleful glare as she folded her arms across her chest.

"You don't need a protector?" he repeated back to her slowly, easing his way through the situation as if he was walking a row of ceiling joists. She wasn't unlocking the door. Had he done something? The hard glassy quality to her hazel eyes and the tight pursing of her lips suggested she was angry at him. Had he pushed her too hard yesterday when he'd asked her about her husband?

Luke leaned a hand on the door frame and gazed at her through the screen, trying to get a clue as to what was going on inside her head. She was still in her nightgown, or at least that was what he thought the sleeveless baby-blue gingham garment she was wearing must be. The narrow ruffled hem just skimmed the tops of her thighs and made his imagination want to go off on several sensual tangents. "Would you care to elaborate?"

"I don't need you to patrol my property like I'm some helpless female. I saw you last night."

''Whoa. You saw me where?''

''In my yard just after midnight. You were looking around. I figured it had to be you or Bill, and he told me it wasn't him, so that leaves you.''

Unease hitched in Luke's chest. ''I don't know how to break this to you, but it wasn't me, either. You're sure you saw someone?''

''Positive.''

''Why didn't you call me?''

''Because I thought it *was* you. Besides, I don't need a pro—''

''Yeah, protector. I got that part.'' Luke clamped down on his temper and stomped off the porch before he blew a gasket. He didn't know why he was so angry. *Yes, he did.* Someone had been snooping around her cottage last night. She could have been attacked or killed, but she hadn't called for help because of that obviously deeply ingrained streak of independence.

Or because of the kind of trouble she was in.

Luke had the queasy feeling that the names of her next-of-kin contacts were as bogus as the phone number she'd given Bill.

''Where are you going?'' Mary called after him.

''I'm looking…for footprints,'' Luke retorted, feeling an irrational satisfaction in throwing her words back in her face.

He half expected the screen door to whip open and Mary to appear, insisting that she could look for footprints on her own, but the door remained tightly shut. She was probably figuring out how to fire him. Luke forced himself to take a few deep breaths and calm down before examining the perimeter of the cottage.

He didn't find any footprints, but a freshly trampled bush beneath her kitchen window suggested someone had been close enough to press his nose against the window. Who? Vacationing teens who'd noticed she was a beautiful young woman living alone? Or someone who intended her harm, like whoever had punctured her tire and thrown the rocks? Luke bet on the latter as he finished circling the cottage and returned to the porch.

Mary stood where he'd left her, her arms wrapped tightly across her chest. He could hear Samantha making cooing noises somewhere inside.

"Find anything?" The strain in her voice drained the remaining traces of anger from his heart. She unhooked the latch on the screen door and allowed him entrance into her home. Samantha was in her playpen, busily punching the knobs and levers on an activity set.

Luke felt helpless in the face of the fear marring Mary's features as he debated what to tell her. Informing her he'd found evidence of a voyeur would only increase the fears she was clearly harboring. And Luke didn't intend to let anyone within peeping range of her windows again, whether she fired him or not. "Did you expect me to?" he asked quietly, suspecting she knew who the voyeur might be.

Mary recoiled from him. "No! Of course not! How could I?" A shudder racked her shoulders, and she combed her fingers through her hair. "I'm sorry. I guess I'm still spooked about the rocks. Do you think it could have been kids again?"

"I thought you only saw one," Luke replied.

"I did, I mean…" She paused, her fingers pressed to her forehead. "I'm sorry, I had a pretty rough night. I saw one person. I couldn't tell if it was a man or woman. I'm assuming it was a man. It could have been someone staying at Shady Pines out for a midnight stroll. Or someone who was mad because Bill made such a fuss about the rock-throwing incident and wanted to get back at me. Maybe whoever was out there thought about toilet-papering my trees or putting eggs in my mailbox, then thought better of it when they realized I was still awake."

"Okay, let's go with that theory. What kids have you seen around the resort in the past few days who are tall enough to be mistaken for a man or a woman at a distance?"

"Well, Alice's older grandchildren, of course, and their assorted friends. Maybe Roger's oldest son, Adam—he's in the cottage next door. There are always a number of kids down at the beach—I'm not certain which cottages they come from. And there are tourists, too. Bill doesn't mind if they stop to picnic as long as they clean up after themselves." Mary frowned. "The only other person I can think of is the ice-cream-cart boy. I don't know his name, but I've met his mother, Donna White, a few times. She sells crafts at the same shops I do. He was a bit short with me when I asked him to give his mother my best while I was buying a juice bar from him at the beach last night after supper, but I think that's just his personality. Anyway, enough of this theorizing. It's summer. Kids goof off. There was no harm done, and we've got some deliveries that need to be made."

Luke found her sudden shift in attitude unsettling. She'd gone from being confrontational and afraid to dismissing the entire episode in the span of a few minutes. Was she trying to convince him or herself that there was nothing to be concerned about?

"Deliveries? You can feel free to make them without me. I'll be fine. I've got plenty of work here to keep me busy for a few hours." He'd be more than fine. He'd take full advantage of being left alone on the premises, provided Mary left the cottage unlocked.

"I'm sure you could manage without me, but I'm too tired to drive, and an extra pair of hands to carry the merchandise into the shops would be much appreciated," Mary said, squelching his plans to snoop. "It's easier said than done to keep an eye on Samantha in her stroller and conduct business."

"And here I thought you wanted my company for my charming personality."

"That, too." A shy smile touched her lips, but it didn't erase the shadows beneath her eyes. "I'm sorry I was so sharp with you earlier."

He shrugged off her apology. "I'm puncture-proof. What needs to be loaded?" Still, the needling suspicion that, contrary to her excuses, she'd never leave him or anyone else alone on her property wormed its way into his thoughts.

While Luke loaded plastic tubs containing the finished crafts into the truck, Shannon packed a diaper bag with snacks and diapers for Samantha, then locked up the cottage.

She didn't realize until they were climbing into the front seat of her truck that asking Luke to drive meant being squished between Samantha's car seat and the bulk of Luke's warm muscled body.

Shannon bit down on her lip as his arm brushed companionably against hers, sending frissons of electricity zinging along the surface of her skin. She tried to distract herself by focusing on the deliveries that needed to be made, telling Luke about the stores she supplied. But each abrupt reply Luke made, punctuated by the shifting of the truck's gears and a subsequent brush of his arm against her body, increased her awareness of his unabated maleness.

Even the sight of his strong capable fingers on the gearshift provoked erotic imaginings that had her blushing to her roots. Why, oh, why had she worn this dress that rode high on her thighs when she sat down? She felt half-naked. Shannon risked looking at Luke's profile to see if he noticed anything amiss. His jaw was locked tight, as if sewn shut with tension. A fine film of perspiration gleamed on his forehead and on the cords of his neck. The wind blowing in from the open driver's-side window ruffled his hair. He glanced at her, his eyes intense and questioning, and Shannon lost her train of thought. If she pressed her lips to his throat, would his skin taste as fiery as the sensations rippling through her?

Loss opened inside her like a dark bottomless pit at the thought of never knowing another man's kiss. Especially Luke's kiss.

Shannon looked away, tears stinging her eyes, as they drove into town. Gold banners printed with the fruits of Blossom Valley fluttered from the old-fashioned light standards. ''Pull over at the curb near the diner," she instructed Luke. "I'll hop out and check my post-office box." With Samantha's car seat blocking the way, it was impossible to climb out the passenger side of the truck. Shannon had no choice but to slide over and accept Luke's hand as he helped her out of the vehicle.

Heat, dry and combustible, blazed through her as their fingers touched, melded. Shannon swayed as the strength of his grip liquefied her limbs. The engine of the truck rumbled unsteadily, mimicking the uneven thrum of her heartbeat.

"Easy now," Luke said, steadying her. The banked desire in his eyes made her breath catch in her lungs and filled her with reassurance that Luke was a man of his word. Nothing more would happen between them unless she allowed it to happen. She drew in a shaky breath and freed her fingers from his grasp. "Do you mind keeping Samantha with you in the truck? I'll check my mailbox and meet you down the street at Glorie's Gifts Galore in a few minutes. If you can find a parking spot in front of the store, it'll be easier to unload."

"No problem, boss. Sammy girl is in good hands."

Shannon cast them an uneasy glance as she walked into the ocher-painted cinder-block building that offered business and mail services. Her box was stuffed with mail, but as she sorted through the envelopes containing bills and catalogs, she didn't find one response to her newspaper ad for a woodworker, which meant she wouldn't be informing Luke she'd hired a permanent replacement for him for at least another week. Maybe longer.

That conclusion elicited a fluttering of mixed emotions in her stomach that she'd just as soon not think about.

Luke had parked her truck two blocks down. From this distance, she could see him on the sidewalk, pulling Samantha's stroller from the bed of the truck.

By the time Shannon reached the same block, he'd removed her daughter from her car seat and was maneuvering her into the stroller as if landing a 747 on an airport runway. Samantha bubbled with laughter as Luke swooped her up and down and finally settled her in the stroller with a plop. Shannon's steps slowed. Maybe someday, she told herself, her daughter would have a father who'd play with her and make her laugh and do all the things a father is supposed to do.

"All set?" Shannon asked, hooking her mailbag over one of the handles of the stroller as Luke finger-combed his hair. "We'll need the mailboxes and the welcome signs for this delivery."

"Sure thing."

"I'll get the door for you." Shannon pushed the stroller toward the red barnlike facade of Glorie's Gifts Galore. To her surprise, the Closed sign hung in the window even though it was midmorning. Shannon found that odd. Glorie was expecting her. The door was locked, but Shannon could see lights on inside. She also saw Glorie on her knees, in tears, amid a path of destruction that looked as if a tornado had swept through the interior of the small shop, scattering debris in all directions. But the foul word spray-painted on the wall behind the cashier hadn't been written by a force of nature.

"OH, MY GOD," Shannon whispered as she hammered on the door to get Glorie's attention.

The plump woman looked up, and when she saw it was Shannon, slowly climbed to her feet and came to the door. Rivulets of mascara traced Glorie's full cheeks and spattered onto the shoulder of her white blouse. "Oh Glorie, what happened?" Shannon asked, opening her arms to embrace the woman.

Glorie's body quivered with shock as she returned Shannon's hug. "Someone broke in last night," she explained in a shaky voice. "The police think he got mad when he didn't find any cash and trashed the place."

"I'm so sorry," Shannon murmured, understanding the woman's terror and feelings of violation. Feelings that Shannon knew took a long time to fade. Glorie would probably feel a sense of anticipatory dread every morning when she opened the shop, just as Shannon tensed every time she entered her cottage, automatically checking for signs that Rob had been there.

She felt the light pressure of a hand on the small of her back and looked up to see Luke behind her. He'd placed a plastic bin containing the letter boxes Glorie had ordered on the sidewalk near the door. He cleared his throat and introduced himself. Glorie withdrew from Shannon's embrace.

"Did you call the police, ma'am?" he asked.

Glorie wiped her face with her fingers, looking dismayed at the smears of mascara that transferred to her fingers.

Shannon handed her a baby wipe from the carryall in the bottom of Samantha's stroller.

"Thank you." Glorie cleaned her fingers and her face. "The police have come and gone. I arrived early this morning and discovered this... The police took some fingerprints, but I don't know if it'll help. So many people come through the shop. I've got to clean up and make a list of the damaged items for the insurance." Glorie's chin wobbled, and her eyes glistened with moisture. "I'm sorry, Mary, but I think some of your crafts took the brunt of the burglar's fury."

Before Shannon could worry over how much lost income would result from the burglary, Glorie assured her that the insurance would cover the damaged inventory. She was just waiting for her daughter to arrive to give her a hand with the clean-up and cataloging.

Shannon decided Glorie could use some company until her daughter arrived. "We've got a couple hours to spare. We'll stay and give you a hand," she offered, exchanging a questioning glance with Luke to make sure he didn't mind, knowing instinctively that he wouldn't feel any more comfortable than she would about leaving Glorie alone to deal with this mess.

"No, I couldn't ask—" Glorie protested.

"You're not asking, we're insisting," Shannon interrupted her with a smile, rubbing the older woman's shoulder. "Just put us to work. Luke, why don't you put Glorie's order back in the truck and we'll deliver it next week."

Glorie planted her fists on her ample hips. "No, no,

I insist on receiving it today as scheduled. I plan to be open for business bright and early tomorrow morning, and I'll need stock. I refuse to lose any of my weekend business over this mishap.''

Bravo! Shannon thought, glad to see the kindly shop owner starting to rally. After Luke carried in the bins from the truck, Glorie dispatched him and Samantha to the hardware store to buy hooks to mount a patchwork quilt over the offensive word marring her wallpaper. Shannon, meanwhile, helped Glorie clear the merchandise from the floor, sorting it by artisan so that Glorie could inspect each piece for damage and catalog it.

Shannon's fingers trembled as she picked up her own work from the debris. Glorie was right—her work had suffered the most, some of the pieces trampled to bits or smashed in half as if broken over a knee.

Even though she knew she'd be compensated for her loss, angry tears filled Shannon's eyes at the wanton destruction.

''Is that all yours?'' Luke inquired softly in her ear as she woefully wrote a list of her ruined work to make Glorie's job easier. She nodded wordlessly, noticing that he'd finished hanging the quilt on the wall behind the cashier. Glorie's shop was looking more put to rights. Samantha was bouncing in her stroller, trying to ring the bell suspended from the front doorknob. Luke touched Shannon's shoulder. ''Uh, did you happen to notice if any of Donna White's crafts were damaged?''

Startled, Shannon glanced up at him. Why would he be concerned if Donna White's crafts were destroyed unless...? Shannon tugged on Luke's wrist, indicating he should follow her as she moved through the store, eyeing the displays they hadn't tackled yet. Now that she thought about it, she hadn't picked up any of Donna White's work from the floor.

Shannon spied several baskets containing hand-painted Christmas ornaments that she was sure were Donna's work.

The baskets were undisturbed. A nearby shelf held a small selection of decorative accent pieces also crafted by Donna. Shannon recognized the crafter's trademark signature. Was it just a coincidence that Donna's work had escaped harm? Shannon slipped a folksy pickle-barrel toothpick holder off the shelf and walked toward Glorie.

"Do you have a pile for Donna White's work?" she asked, holding up the toothpick holder that had been marked down to half price. "This seems to have survived intact."

"Wouldn't ya know it?" Glorie groaned, shaking her head as she reached for the item. "I'd have liked to see the last of this. Donna has original ideas, but I'm having a tough time selling her pieces for the prices she wants. I finally stopped ordering from her last month."

"Oh." Shannon felt a rash of goosebumps rise along her arms. She didn't like what she was thinking. The loss of Glorie's retail support must have affected Donna's income. Had Donna's son felt resentful enough to retaliate on his mother's behalf? Could he have been Shannon's midnight prowler?

UNEASE COILED like strands of barbed wire around
Luke's limbs. He was a big-city cop, but he didn't for
a minute believe that the vandalism in Glorie's shop
was the result of a burglar frustrated that he didn't take
in a bigger haul. The store was on the town's main
street. Even in the middle of the night there would be
occasional traffic or a patrol car going by that might
spot movement inside the store or hear the sounds of
the devastation taking place. It took time to create a
mess like this, and most burglars were in and out in a
matter of minutes. The ones who brought cans of spray
paint or marked the scene with urine or feces felt a
need to leave their signature. Luke particularly didn't
like the fact that Mary's work seemed to have suffered
the most. Or that it had been destroyed with such rage.
The same kind of rage that might prompt someone to
puncture a car tire or hide in the bushes stalking a lone
female.

At the moment Donna White's son ranked promi-
nently at the top of Luke's suspect list. While it was
tempting to ask Glorie if she'd ever met Donna
White's son or knew the boy's name, Luke held back
and changed the subject to prevent Mary from probing
any further, as well. Better to pass the information to
the investigating officer and let him run with it. But
before he could approach the local police, Luke had
to level with Mary about her flat tire and the trampled
bushes outside her home.

By the time Glorie's daughter arrived, Samantha
had grown tired of exploring the store and had eaten
all the snacks Mary had brought. Mary reluctantly admitted that Samantha needed to go home for her nap.

She gave Glorie another hug and promised to call later in the afternoon.

"You think Donna's son did it, too, don't you?" Mary said as she strapped Samantha into her car seat and gave her a bottle of juice.

Luke held the door open for her so she could slide into the front seat, stalwartly keeping his eyes averted from the acres of leg that thing she called a dress exposed. "Looks that way."

Mary paused on the edge of the driver's seat, her beautiful lightly tanned limbs turned toward him, looking feminine and vulnerable. The thought of some kid peeping through her windows in the middle of the night brought a sharp twist of revulsion to his belly. "So why are we keeping this secret from Glorie? Surely she has a right to know."

Luke looked down into the maelstrom of confusion in Mary's eyes. He still didn't know who this woman was or whether or not she was using his wife's identity for her personal gain, but he didn't want anything to happen to her. "I want to help Glorie just as much as you do," he said mildly. "But there's something I haven't told you, and I think you should know it before we do anything."

Her body grew deathly still. "You're scaring me."

Against his will, Luke's knuckles grazed her cheek. "I'm sorry. I probably should have said something sooner. That day I changed your tire I noticed that it had been cut. Deliberately. And this morning, when I took a look around your cottage, I found the bushes beneath the kitchen window were trampled."

The muscles in Mary's neck convulsed, and a glassy mask of anger slipped over her face.

Shannon struggled for control, trying not to give in to the fear expanding in her and forcing her heart into her throat. She'd checked Luke out; he was who he said he was. She couldn't think of one logical reason he would have kept such information to himself unless her ex-husband had hired him to get close to her. Rob could be so likable and convincing. Maybe he'd persuaded Luke that he was a concerned ex-husband and father. It sounded farfetched, but Shannon was in a position to believe the inconceivable.

All her maternal protective instincts urged her to proceed with caution, while her heart argued vociferously that Luke would never harm her or her daughter. She could reason with him. "You're right," she replied, trying to curb the frostiness in her tone. "You should have mentioned this sooner. Why didn't you?"

"Because I didn't want to frighten you further. When I was in high school, a new family moved in next door to us. There was a little girl about six and a boy of ten. We used to find them hiding in my mother's garden or in my old treehouse—"

"I don't see what that has to do with me or why you kept your suspicions to yourself," Shannon snapped, instantly regretting her sharp reply when Samantha pulled the bottle out of her mouth and whimpered, her brows drawn together over wide puzzled eyes. "I'm sorry, baby." Shannon leaned over and soothed her daughter with soft promises of a nap and a story. "We shouldn't be discussing this now in front of her. We'll talk about it later, okay?"

Luke didn't answer. But he slid into the truck beside her and put the key in the ignition. Instead of starting the engine, he stared out the window at the side mirror. "When we found those kids hiding on our property," he said softly, "they always had this hunted look in their eyes. They begged us not to tell their father where they were. They were running scared about something—usually their father's violent temper. They didn't want to know that their father was calling every-one in the neighborhood looking for them, or that he was cussing a blue streak and threatening to whip them if they didn't come home. They just wanted to know when he left for work so that it was safe to go home."

Shannon closed her eyes against the horrible images his words evoked. Why was he telling her this? Did he know something? She flinched as his fingers cupped her chin and gently forced her to turn and look at him. He was too close, the warm solid feel of his body offering her shelter, the compassion evident in his eyes eroding the defensive shield she was trying desperately to maintain. Luke's voice thickened with emotion. "You have that same hunted look in your eyes, Mary, which tells me you're running scared, too. I just want to help if you'll let me."

Hot tears scalded her eyes as something shifted in-side Shannon that gave her battered soul restored faith in the goodness of others. In the goodness of Luke, who was willing to come to her aid.

Her cheek muscles ached from trying to keep her emotions in check. From resisting the overwhelming urge to share with a friend the burden she'd been liv-ing under. To feel the solace that Luke's arms would offer. "What happened to those children?" she whispered, neither confirming nor denying his observation.

"My mother reported them to the authorities. The children were taken out of the home, and the husband beat his wife black and blue for telling tales to the neighbors. We never heard of them again or what became of their children." He paused, and Shannon's heart withered. She could guess what had most likely happened to that poor woman and her children.

"Are you going to let me help you, Mary?" Luke pressed after a heartbeat had passed. "Have other things happened to you that make you think someone is trying to hurt you?"

Chapter Six

"Just phone calls."

Luke prayed those few words would be the first pebbles to fall in what would amount to an avalanche of information. "What kind of phone calls?"

"Wrong numbers, I think. They never say anything. They just stay on the line and listen while I ask repeatedly who's calling. I hang up as soon as I realize they aren't going to respond."

"How many calls like this have you received?"

"Recently?" Mary looked decidedly uncomfortable. "Would you mind driving while we talk? I really want to get Samantha home for her nap, and I still have two deliveries to make along the way." She gave him a hard look when he didn't react. "The last time I checked, I was still your boss. Turn right at the next intersection and head down to the park by the lake. There's a restaurant overlooking the lake called The Gazebo that has a small gift shop for tourists. They sell a lot of my crow plant pokes."

Luke realized she was trying to pull rank on him to end the conversation. But he could drive and press her for more answers at the same time. He started the truck and checked his mirrors before pulling onto Main Street. "So, how many phone calls have you received in the past month?"

"I'm not sure."

Luke gave her a sidelong glance that told her he didn't believe her.

Mary sighed. "Okay, three that I remember in the last week or so. One was late at night when I was working. The other two were during the day. But I don't understand why he's venting his anger on me. I don't have anything to do with Glorie's business decisions. She buys what she thinks she can sell."

"Maybe he views you as his mother's competition—the newcomer who came into town and took sales away from her. Didn't you say you spotted the prowler as you were finishing up last night? You do most of your painting at night, don't you? Maybe he was spying on you in hopes of stealing some of your product designs."

"It was after midnight when I saw the prowler. You're suggesting that he left my cottage and drove into town, then trashed Glorie's store?"

Luke hung a right at the intersection. "He might have done it the other way around, but yes, that's exactly what I'm suggesting. I think he slit the tire and threw rocks at you, too. Maybe to frighten you, make your life difficult. Maybe because it makes him feel powerful to torment you, or maybe he thinks he can scare you into going back to wherever you came from."

Mary slumped against the seat, her brow furrowed. Luke halted at a stop sign, checking the traffic behind him. At the end of the street a small lake glistened like a dab of wet paint. "The kid needs to have his criminal career nipped in the bud before he hurts someone."

She tensed like a cat arching its back. "What do you mean?"

Luke eased slowly down the street past yellowing lawns, searching for the restaurant. "You'll have to go to the police and tell them what's been happening to you. Let them decide if there's any connection between those events and the vandalism at Glorie's gift shop."

"And tell them what, specifically? About a few wrong numbers and a trampled bush. A raccoon or a dog could have trampled that bush. You told me you didn't see any footprints."

His fingers grew clammy on the steering wheel. Why on earth was she being so unreasonable and argumentative? "What about the tire?"

"No offense, but it's only your opinion that the tire was slashed."

Luke pulled over to the side of the road, trying to keep his temper in check. A blue sedan blasted by them with a toot of its horn, followed by three other vehicles.

He watched the other vehicles pass, counting slowly under his breath.

"The Gazebo's closer to the lake on the left," Mary said. "It's set back among the willow—"

"Forget about the restaurant! How about we let the police decide whether or not your tire was slashed? It's still in the back of your truck, isn't it?"

"Luke, please keep driving. I really need to deliver my stock." Tension vibrated in the cab like strands of brittle beads. "We don't have any proof that Donna's son did any of these things."

"Whatever you say, boss." Luke put his foot on the gas and gunned the engine, zipping into the other lane to pass a green sedan that was parking on the shoulder.

"Thank you." A sliver of a smile etched Mary's lips. One that seemed to mock him and continue to deny him the truth.

Don't press too hard. Luke pulled into the drive of a beautifully restored lakeside house with a wide deep porch that was used for alfresco dining. Most of the tables were occupied at this hour of the day. The gazebo, for which the restaurant was named, was an iron fretwork structure twined with masses of pink roses that was plopped like the top tier of a wedding cake in the center of a formal garden with white gravel paths that swept down to the lake. He angled into a parking spot beneath a shade tree and cut the engine. "Just at least consider it, please."

Mary nudged him with her elbow. "I am considering it. Now let me out."

Luke reluctantly climbed out of the truck, holding the door for her and straddling an invisible line between his personal need for justice and his duty as a police officer to serve and protect. Mary needed protection from whomever or whatever was threatening her. He thrust the box containing the plant pokes into her hands and tried one more time. "Does the gift shop in there carry Donna White's designs?"

"I'm not sure."

"Then make it your business to find out. It's possible they stopped carrying her crafts, too."

SHE WAS BEHAVING abominably. Shannon chastised herself as she marched up the crisply painted porch steps carrying the box of plant pokes. An urge curled through her like a velvet voice, wheedling with her to turn back and tell Luke...what?

She couldn't tell him the truth. Not now. Not ever. Just like she couldn't go to the police and report what had been happening to her. She couldn't risk the attention. If the police were going to link Donna White's son to the burglary at Glorie's gift boutique, they'd have to do it without her assistance. She couldn't have them asking questions about her, looking into her background, asking her to testify.

She couldn't add perjuring herself to her list of crimes. The tantalizing smells of pasta and fresh-baked bread from The Gazebo's kitchen made Shannon feel nauseous. The velvet voice slithered around her heart. *What if it isn't the boy who's tormenting you?*

Her legs wobbled unsteadily. Shannon eased in through the wide French door and dropped into a cushioned wicker chair near the hostess's podium. The air conditioner was working full blast inside, chilling her blood and numbing her mind. She needed time to think, and sort the facts from the conjecture. Just what were real and what were imagined threats?

She tried to list them all in her mind. The phone calls. The rock attack. Should she include the baby rattle that she'd found on the windshield the other day?

She hadn't imagined the prowler last night, but with the exception of the rock attack, the other incidents could be easily explained coincidences. And the tire...could she take it to a garage and have an outside opinion?

Shannon grasped on to the idea. She wasn't running until she had solid evidence that Rob was here in Blossom Valley. The annoying phone calls and the prowling were true-to-form Rob, but why would he slit her tire? She and Samantha could have been killed. Was that supposed to be her punishment for leaving him?

"Can I help you?"

Shannon started. A hostess was beaming at her. "Would you like a table, miss, or are you waiting for the rest of your party?"

The box nearly slid from her lap. Shannon clutched it like a buoy holding her afloat. "No, th-thank you. I'm making a delivery to the gift shop. I just felt a little dizzy when I stepped inside. Probably the abrupt change in temperature. It's blistering outside."

"I'll bring you a glass of water. You look pale."

Shannon felt ashamed. One more kind stranger, like Luke, concerned for her welfare. She didn't deserve it. "No, I'm fine, really." She pushed herself out of the wicker chair, telling herself that she *would* be fine once she got some answers. And the gift shop seemed like the logical place to start.

SHANNON CRADLED the information the gift-shop manager had told her like a firefly ensnared in her cupped hands, unsure whether or not to share it with Luke. As she approached the truck, she heard Luke's voice drifting toward her, masculine and rumbling like a wagon wheel bumping over a cobblestone street. ''And then the lion said to the elephant...''

He was telling Samantha a story.

Shannon felt a part of her heart break off and drop to her stomach with a splash. Heaven help her, she could fall in love with this man.

Ha! She was halfway there already, she ruefully admitted as the driver's door opened and Luke materialized before her, so solid and dependable-looking she wanted to tear off the navy T-shirt and strip him of those faded jeans and lose herself in the muscled contours of his body. Satisfy the desire teeming just beneath the surface of her skin to know his kiss.

Luke's jaw tensed as their gazes collided, then he leaned into the cab, talking to her daughter, ''Look, Sammy girl, here's Mommy.''

Mommy.

He spoke as if they were a family. A wish swelled in her throat, as if denied entrance to her heart by barred gates. ''Did she miss me?''

''We both did.''

Shannon told herself he didn't mean anything by that as she scrambled past him onto the seat, but her elbow, where he gripped it, assisting her, warmed as if dipped in a hot pool. Samantha gave her a drowsy yawn, showing the two pearly buds in her gums. Shannon showered her with attention while Luke started the truck. They had one delivery to make at a fruit stand on the highway south of town.

She gave Luke directions, then before he could ask, she told him that The Gazebo's gift shop hasn't carried

Donna White's crafts since Christmas. "And Donna's son's name is Dylan. But that still doesn't mean I think we should go to the police."

Luke didn't react, which made her wonder if he was even listening. He turned left at the next street into a small subdivision, instead of proceeding straight to the corner. "You're going the wrong way," Shannon informed him.

"Nope, I'm making a detour. I think we're being followed."

He stopped her before her head could whip around. "Look in the rearview mirror. See the green car? I noticed it when we were driving to The Gazebo. It pulled off the road when we did. And here it is again right behind us."

Shannon's heart started to pound. A luxury sage-green sedan had pulled into the subdivision at a crawl, but she lost sight of it as Luke made another quick turn.

"Does the car look familiar?"

"No. What are we going to do?"

Catch him. Luke made a U-turn, whipping the truck around like a police cruiser. "We're going to try to get a look at him and get the license plate. Hold on."

Luke caught a quick glimpse of thick forearms and salt-and-pepper hair slicked back from a high forehead as the other vehicle went past, the driver stomping the gas pedal to the floor when he realized he'd been made. Luke went after him in controlled pursuit, aware of the possibility that children could be playing nearby. Something about the suspect seemed vaguely familiar. All Luke needed was a plate number to identify him.

"Don't you dare follow him, Luke! Not with my daughter in the car!" Mary's shrill terrified tone put a damper on the adrenaline pumping through his veins. A few more seconds and he'd be close enough to read it...

"Read me the plate number," he ordered her.

Mary rattled off the tag. "We've got it. Let him go. *Now.*"

Luke kept the gas pedal depressed just long enough to ensure that he read the plate number for himself. Then he backed off, reducing his speed to the posted limit.

Mary's fingers were embedded in the dashboard, her knuckles white. Her voice trembled with unleashed fury. "I should fire you. That was foolish and reckless. Somebody could have gotten hurt."

"I had no intention of catching up with him. I just wanted the license-plate number," he said calmly. "It definitely wasn't Dylan." He described the man he'd seen, hoping his subconscious would dredge up more details that might help him place the face. "Anyone you know?"

Mary's mouth gaped. The freckles stood out on her nose and cheeks like specks of nutmeg, making her appear very young. And uncertain. A fleeting expression of relief rolled over her fine-boned features before she could compose herself. "Doesn't ring any bells."

"Are you sure? I only got a glimpse of him, but I think I've seen him somewhere before—maybe around town."

"I'm positive."

Luke brooded over her response, not wanting to hear what his ears so plainly told him. Why would she be relieved that Dylan hadn't been driving the car? As he frequently did while working his beat, Luke turned his observation around, trying to look at it from another angle. Was Mary relieved because she'd expected the driver to be someone else and it wasn't?

A leaden weight settled on his chest as he turned onto Main Street. Why did he have the niggling keep-your-back-to-the-wall feeling that something important was just out of his grasp? Maybe his thought processes were dulled by the undercurrent of awareness created by the softness of the thigh pressed to his flank and the sweetly disarming scent of Mary's hair.

"Do you think it could have been another relative of Donna White's—or perhaps a friend?" Mary's suggestion was offered timidly, like a dinner invitation to an unexpected and unwanted guest. Polite, but lacking the ring of sincerity.

"There's an easy way to find out. We can stop by the nearest police station and ask them to identify the owner of the vehicle."

He felt immediate resistance rise from her like a wall of wind, pushing back at him. "*No.* We've already been over this. It's my life and my decision. If anything is said or done, it will be privately. Blossom Valley is a small town. We can probably find out who the owns the car by asking around."

Luke grit his teeth in frustration. "Why are you being stubborn about this? We were being followed! The person driving that car could have the intent to

do you bodily harm. What if he intended to slit one
of your tires again?'' *Or worse.* Luke thought of his
own wife pulled from her car at a dark intersection
and beaten savagely.

Mary clenched her fingers in her lap. Luke wanted
to snatch up her hands and plead with her to listen,
but he kept his hands on the steering wheel. ''You
sound like a cop.''

Luke tensed, every atom in his body on full alert.
Had he inadvertently blown his cover?

''Donna's a single mother like me,'' Mary plowed
on, apparently not giving serious thought to her statement. ''Dylan—if he's involved in this—probably
thinks he's protecting his mother's source of income.
Having Dylan arrested will only exacerbate Donna's
problems. Maybe all we need to do is give Dylan a
hint that we know what's going on and it will all
stop.''

''But—''

''Luke, promise me. This stays between us.''

Luke said the words. But it was a promise he didn't
intend to keep.

Chapter Seven

Shannon pressed the heels of her palms to her throbbing temples and tried to think. She'd dismissed Luke for the day when they'd arrived back at her cottage twenty minutes ago, giving him the impression that she intended to lie down and nap with Samantha. But as soon as the baby-sitter she'd called arrived, she planned to drive back to town to have that tire looked at. And ask a few questions of the mechanics at the local garage. She figured men who worked on cars probably paid more attention than most to who was driving what in Blossom Valley. Maybe she'd get lucky and find out whom that car belonged to.

But the prospect of going into town behind Luke's back made her feel inexplicably guilty. Should she call him and invite him to join her? She owed him nothing, no explanations, no loyalty. But she was unhappy with the way things had been left unsettled between them when they'd parted company. Maybe she'd just call him. He'd be the first to admit he was wrong if it turned out that tire hadn't been slashed. Shannon walked into the kitchen to the phone and dialed Luke's number. The phone rang a dozen times before she hung up.

Shannon peeked into Samantha's room, reassured by the sound of Samantha's soft even breathing.

A tap on the screen door had her turning around, her heartbeat skittering at the thought it might be Luke. It was Julie, Alice Nesbitt's oldest grandchild, a responsible fourteen-year-old with thick tangled cords of blond hair a mermaid would envy and a shy smile that attempted to hide the braces she deplored.

Since Julie had sat with Samantha on other occasions, Shannon went over the basics, then reached for her purse and keys and headed out the door. She was halfway across the lawn toward the driveway when she changed course and headed for the path that led to Luke's cottage and the beach. She imagined he hadn't answered when she'd called earlier because he was sitting outside enjoying his lunch or had decided to head down to the beach for a swim. But when Abner's dilapidated cottage came into view, she saw that Luke's car was gone.

Where had he gone in such a hurry?

Had he decided to get a few answers for himself, just as she had?

Shannon spun on her heel and started to run back to her truck. He'd given her word that he wouldn't go to the police. But what if he'd lied?

SHANNON TREMBLED with rage and dread when she saw Luke's car in the parking lot of the RCMP detachment. On the drive into town she'd told herself that he wouldn't betray her, that he was a man who kept his word and his promises, that he'd probably decided to research his plans to open his own business this afternoon...or had gone into town for groceries. The sight of his blue sedan wounded her like a physical blow.

But maybe it wasn't his car. She'd never made note of his license-plate number.

She'd have to go inside and find out. Her lungs refused to draw in air as she marched toward the detachment office. Even when she saw Luke's tall lean form, his hip propped against the information desk where he was speaking to an officer, she still didn't want to believe it.

Her fingers were rubbery as she struggled to open the heavy glass door. It rattled as it closed behind her.

Luke turned at the sound. Guilt, black and tormented as the thoughts she was entertaining, flashed in his eyes as their gazes met.

How much had he told them?

"Luke?"

Luke groaned inwardly, hearing the hurt in Mary's voice underscoring his name. He tried to compartmentalize his emotions so he could focus on the task at hand. But the silent accusation in Mary's hazel eyes slipped past the barrier and pierced his emotions, making him feel things he didn't want to feel. *Shouldn't* feel for this woman.

Had she changed her mind and decided to come forward, or had she followed him here to prevent him from talking to the police?

He took two steps toward her. "I'm glad you decided to join me, Mary. The car that was following us was reported stolen three days ago.''

Her jaw was set rigidly as her face blanched. ''Stolen?'' She glanced at Staff Sergeant Rayford, the detachment commander, then back at Luke as if coming to some kind of decision. Luke's heart clanged like a warning bell. He wanted to reach into her and pull out hand over fist the secrets she was afraid to unburden.

Tell me, he silently implored her, feeling an inexplicable sense of foreboding that both her future and his depended on what transpired in the next few minutes. Only she held the key to his unanswered questions. And what if they weren't the answers he needed?

Then he'd spend the rest of his life hoping for another lead in his wife's murder.

Her voice lowered, pleading and desperate. ''May I speak to you privately, please?''

''Excuse us a moment.'' Luke nodded to the watch commander, whose hooded gaze was fixed speculatively on Mary in a way that made Luke want to shield her from the sergeant's view. Rayford knew he was here working on a murder investigation, though he didn't know the details of the case. Luke took Mary's elbow, intending to guide her into a quiet corner of the room. Her body quivered with tension from his touch like a fine crystal goblet reacting to the clink of a spoon.

''Not here. Outside,'' Mary insisted.

She moved quickly, a half step ahead of him out of the building and into the unmerciful heat of the day. Luke felt his skin heat as if struck by thousands of matches lit simultaneously. Mary made a beeline for her truck, her sandals slapping against the asphalt. Luke waited for her to say something, sweat already beading at his temples.

She wheeled around, squaring to face him, her hands bunched on her hips, strands of blond hair sticking to her damp face like a crown of thorns. "You broke your promise and you lied to me."

"Guilty as charged," he acknowledged harshly, curling his fingers into his palms to keep himself from touching her. "And I'd do it again because I would never forgive myself if something happened to you or your daughter. There's something wrong here. I can feel it like a hand gripping my throat. And if you won't help yourself, then I will."

He stared down at her, hating her secrets and wanting her physically—even when she looked sick with fear—in a way that shamed him.

"Okay." She spoke so softly he barely heard her.

"Okay what?" he asked patiently.

Her lids closed over her hazel eyes—in surrender? Or resignation? She exhaled a shaky breath, one hand fumbling to lift the flap of her purse. "Okay, I'll tell you, but I don't want to talk here. Somewhere else…" She produced her keys from her purse and handed them to him.

Luke closed his fingers around the keys, hope rising through him. "Let's go to the park by the lake."

CHOICES. CHOICES. Why did life keep hurtling difficult choices at you, as if you were a batter at the plate facing a pitcher determined to strike you out?

Shannon hadn't ever wanted to be in the game, much less be pulled into a never-ending tournament for which peace seemed the prized trophy. And her third strike had just sailed over the plate. The car that had been following them had been stolen, and she couldn't shake from her mind the glint of pride in Rob's eyes when he'd boasted of stealing cars and going joy-riding with his friends in his youth.

Granted, the man Luke described hadn't sounded like Rob, but then, Rob might have altered his appearance to lessen his visibility. Or maybe his black hair had become threaded with gray in the past sixteen months.

And now she was faced with that awful decision again. If it was Rob, she'd have to run. And she couldn't manage her escape alone this time. Not with a baby and a business to consider and the possibility that Rob could be watching her every move. She'd need someone she could trust to assist her.

Someone like Luke.

She should be angry with him for going to the police behind her back—without a word of apology— but she wasn't. He'd demonstrated a depth of caring for her and her daughter that made her want to weep at the thought of saying goodbye to him.

Luke parked the truck in the shade of a huge willow and turned off the engine. Shannon heard a pinging sound as the engine stilled, ticks marking off a countdown. There was no delaying this any longer. In fact, it would be a relief to tell him. She'd been carrying the burden alone for too long.

Shannon climbed out of the truck, waiting for Luke

to join her beneath the canopy of the willow. His arms circled her waist from behind in an embrace that made her feel both cherished and secure. He leaned down so that his chin tucked into the curve of her neck, the stubble of his cheek lightly abrading her skin, before he brought his mouth to her ear. "This better?"

His warm breath tickled her ear, awakening her to sensations she hadn't felt in years. Her laugh turned into a strangled sob. "Better" was an understatement. "Heaven" was more apt a description as Luke's arms tightened around her, molding her fully against him, his fingers splaying over her belly.

"Start at the beginning," he advised.

The beginning? Shannon rested against him, wanting to melt into the warmth and rock-hard strength of his body as a tear trickled down her cheek. Bitterness welled in her, nearly choking her. "I lied to you about my husband," she began. "I'm not a widow. I'm divorced, and I think the man you saw in that car was my ex-husband stalking me. Again."

LUKE LISTENED as Mary's story tumbled out, careful not to interrupt or judge, only desiring to soak it all in as Mary told it in her own way, at her own pace.

"I'm originally from Halifax. I met Rob when he was hired as a consultant to plan a conference for the government department I was working in at the time. I was a coordinator of research and planning. Rob was so successful. He entered a room with all this dynamic energy, sort of like an arrogant maître d' whose arrogance only makes him appear distinguished and oddly charming. The day after we met at a planning meeting, he sent me flowers and invited me out to dinner. It was so flattering. I'd never had that kind of attention before from a man. My other dating experiences had been ordinary in comparison. Before I knew it, we were having dinner together three or four nights a week.''

Mary tensed in his arms. ''Things happened very fast. We got married four months after we met. It was so magical—inside the fort on Citadel Hill in Halifax. Rob pulled the ceremony together in an amazingly short amount of time and even hired a stage crew to create a light snowfall. We honeymooned in France for two weeks. I felt so lucky to have such a wonderfully attentive and romantic husband. I was too in love to notice things that should have been warning signals.''

Luke emotionally braced himself.

''A friend of my mother's, Clarissa, owned a craft/ tea shop in Peggy's Cove. When I was in high school I worked for her on weekends, learning how to tole paint—that's a decorative paint technique using patterns—and make crafts, which she sold. Then I kept it up as a hobby through university, designing my own things to sell in Clarissa's shop in my spare time. Rob and I had been married almost three months when Clarissa called and asked me to come by the shop; she had something special she wanted to talk to me about. My mother had told her that Rob and I were talking about my quitting work and starting a family. She wanted to know if I would be interested in taking on a part-time job teaching tole-painting. I was so thrilled! This was my dream job.

"I accepted right on the spot and hurried home to make a special dinner to celebrate. I cooked all of Rob's favorite foods—which should have told me something about our relationship if I'd taken the time to examine it. Anyway, when I told Rob my news, he…" Mary paused and Luke felt a tremor work through her shoulders to her thighs. "He hit me."

Luke swallowed hard, anger rearing in him at the way she bowed her head as if ashamed.

"He hit me here, and here and here." As she spoke, she touched her face, her chest and then laid her hand beside his on her abdomen. Luke laced his fingers through hers.

"I'm sorry," he whispered hoarsely.

"I walked out on him. Thank God he didn't try to stop me." Her voice shook. "I think he believed he had so much control over me that it never occurred to him I wouldn't come back." Her chin lifted defiantly, filling Luke with admiration for her. "But I didn't. I went to a doctor, then the police. Then I called a lawyer and I filed for divorce."

Good girl. She'd had the courage to get out. Luke had seen far too many women, bruised and in denial, stuck in the same abusive cycle.

"Thankfully another case was adjourned and we got their court date, and the divorce was just over a month later. But every day leading up to the divorce he called me at work several times a day. I told him I had nothing to say to him and hung up. Fortunately security in the government offices is tight, and that prevented him from entering the building, but it didn't stop him from waiting for me outside on the street with flowers and once with a musician playing a violin. He even found out where my new apartment was and bombarded me with notes and gifts, and messages on my answering machine, begging me to give our marriage another chance.'' She laughed awkwardly, but Luke heard the hollow ring of desperation in her tone.

''Of course, that was the last thing I wanted to do. My lawyer had advised me to press charges against Rob for the assault, not that it did any good. His trial took place two weeks after our divorce hearing. He was given a three-year suspended sentence, which meant he had to do three years' probation, instead of going to jail. And he was ordered to do some community service and to attend anger-management classes. There was a No Communications Order as a condition of his probation, too. He wasn't supposed to contact me or my family. His probation officer called me and told me to notify him if Rob made any contact with me or my family.''

Luke remained silent, suspecting Rob hadn't respected the No Communications Order.

Mary picked up the thread of her story. ''I got a transfer to another department in a city about an hour outside of Halifax and moved in with a co-worker's sister, but he found me again. That's when things started getting a little scary. Somehow he got into the apartment and went through my belongings. I'd discover things out of place—a book of love poems in my lingerie drawer, love notes that Rob had given me during our courtship in the pockets of my clothing. Once I came home to find our wedding photo on the table beside my bed. Of course, I couldn't prove he'd entered as there was no sign of forced entry.

"I quit my job and moved again, this time to Sydney, which was a good five hours away. I shared a house with a friend of a friend. I was so careful—I didn't even have a phone listing and all the utilities were listed in my roommate's name. I took a job as an administrative assistant in a cheesecake factory, thinking Rob couldn't possibly find me there, but he did." Her last words were quietly spoken, fateful.

Luke waited, wondering how her story was going to end, puzzling over missing pieces. His admiration for her strength of character grew word by painfully uttered word.

"One morning I found one of our wedding photos beneath the windshield wiper of my car. Rob had torn his image out of the photo, then scratched up my face. The same day he sent flowers to me at work, along with a note apologizing for ruining the photo and blaming me for making him angry. I called his probation officer and left messages to report both incidents. Then just before closing time, a limousine drove up outside the factory, and Rob emerged in a tuxedo." She hesitated, and Luke could hear the hitch in her breath.

"He can be very smooth and persuasive. Apparently he informed the front-desk person he was picking me up for a romantic dinner. A supervisor told him there was no one working here by my name and insisted he leave. Rob lost his temper and called me a few choice words, demanding I appear. He'd completed his anger-therapy classes and thought that entitled him to another chance.'' She made a wry face. ''I don't think the classes helped. A couple of employees restrained him until the police arrived and placed him under arrest.''

Mary sighed. ''He was charged with stalking and violating his probation. He was convicted, though he only spent eight months in prison, instead of his year's sentence. They let him out early for good behavior. I wanted to make sure he couldn't find me when he got out, so I moved again, this time out of the province. My mother, my aunt and I were so careful. We didn't want anyone to know where I'd gone. We suspected that Rob had broken into their home in order to find my address in Sydney.''

A gust of wind rippled through the veil of leaves surrounding them. Mary shuddered in Luke's arms. ''I had a job in a shop, selling ladies' clothes,'' she continued. ''Once a week I'd treat myself to dinner out, then go home with a movie rental or a craft project. Two weeks after Rob's release from prison he showed up at the restaurant where I was dining and asked if he could join me.''

Self-reproach rang in her voice. ''This probably sounds really stupid, but I let him stay. I think the fight had gone out of me, seeing him appear like that—a nightmare that refused to go away. He was violating the conditions of his probation and I should have called the police, but I didn't because he said he understood now that our marriage was over and he only wanted to talk to me for a few minutes so he could have some closure to our relationship. Then he promised to leave.'' Her head bowed again. ''It sounded like such a reasonable request. And it struck me that maybe I'd brought this situation on myself by refusing to talk to him or acknowledge his overtures. I hadn't spoken to him since I'd walked out of our home that night, thinking there was nothing to say that could excuse the unforgivable, but maybe that had only served to enrage him, make him even more determined than ever to get some response from me.''

"You weren't responsible for his hitting you," Luke said roughly, unable to restrain himself any longer. It tore him in two to see her blaming herself for being victimized.

"No, but I made the decision to let him join me at my table for drinks. Even then, he continued to fool me. He was so sincere and contrite part of me was desperate enough to be rid of him that I wanted to believe his apology for destroying our marriage. He told me he loved me and then he left...and...'' Mary's breath caught on a sob.

Luke pressed a kiss into her scented hair, wishing he could blank the months and years of terror from her life. She didn't deserve any of this. No woman did. "Go on," he encouraged her.

"And I went home and then, nothing. I woke up the next morning feeling very strange, as if I'd woken from an unpleasant dream, but I couldn't remember the dream. I kept expecting Rob to show up, or that I'd find evidence he'd been inside my apartment. I thought the stress of waiting for him to reappear with a vengeance was making me ill. I went to see my doctor. That's when I found out I was pregnant. I couldn't see how that could possibly be—I hadn't been with anyone. Hadn't even considered dating. I thought my doctor must have made some kind of mistake until she asked me if I frequented bars or restaurants and described a date-rape drug that produces a sedative effect and amnesia in its victims.''

Luke heard a roaring in his ears like thunder rumbling in the distance. He was familiar with the drug, knew it was used in high schools and college campuses. ''You think Rob put the drug in your drink the night he met you at the restaurant?''

Mary didn't hesitate. ''The dates fit. I'm sure he followed me home.''

Luke was at a loss for words, enraged and sorrowed by what must have happened that fateful night, and awed by her courage. It took a woman of incredible strength to walk away from her marriage and stand up to an abusive husband. Mary had endured all that and still had the compassion to embrace a child forced on her in an act of violence. Luke swore to himself he wouldn't rest until he made sure Rob was no longer a threat to Mary and her daughter. ''I'm sorry this happened to you....''

''I'm so glad I don't remember any of it,'' she whispered. ''And I don't regret Samantha.''

''And you never will—she's so much your daughter...'' Luke felt a part of him bind to her as he turned her in his arms, needing to see her eyes. Were they empty of secrets now? Her story explained so much, but there was no apparent connection to his wife. And she wouldn't be the first suspect to bend the truth to her advantage. Still, she'd given him enough details that he could corroborate her identity once he knew her husband's name. While he was disappointed and frustrated at hitting another dead end in his wife's murder investigation, he was also relieved. The awareness that he need feel no guilt for enjoying Mary in his arms stole through him quietly, serendipitously. "Everything's going to be okay. I'm not going to let anybody get near you or Samantha until we figure out what's going on and who's behind this."

Mary laid a hand on his chest and Luke felt his heart leap toward her palm. "I can't believe this is happening again. I can't be one hundred percent certain that Rob has been playing these pranks, though I do know he and some friends stole cars as a means of recreation in their youth. The man you described driving the green car could have been him in some kind of disguise. Rob's hair was completely black last time I saw him. But I did find a baby rattle tucked beneath the windshield of my truck the same morning my tire went flat."

Luke frowned, mentally examining this revelation as if it was the only piece of evidence bagged at a crime scene. "You didn't mention that before."

"I didn't think it was important until this morning when you told me you thought someone had cut the tire deliberately and been camped outside my window last night. I was planning to go to the garage and have the tire checked by an expert this afternoon." Sheepish splotches of color stained her cheeks. "I admit, I wasn't going to invite you along originally, but I changed my mind after you went home. That's when I discovered you'd pulled a disappearing act yourself.

I had a hunch you'd gone to the police station." Her tone was slightly accusatory.

Luke couldn't find fault with her for her instincts. He gently gripped her shoulders. "At least now I understand why you were reluctant to go to the police concerning Dylan's possible involvement in the burglary at Glorie's gift shop."

"I didn't want to falsely accuse anyone. And I still don't. I have no proof that Rob is in the area. Believe me, Luke, I've been through the court process twice before, for what little good it did me. And this time I have something more precious to lose. Do you think I want to go on record saying that I believe Rob is the father of my child? I have no evidence that he raped me. I *invited* him to join me at the restaurant. What if he takes it into his head to sue for custody or visitation? Now do you see why I don't want to go to the police unless I've seen him with my own eyes?"

"He might have already slit your tire. What if he ups the ante and shows up intending to kill you and Samantha?" Luke demanded, struggling with the brutal reality that stalkers were more likely to kill their victims when they reached a point where they felt they'd lost them. Often a stalker reached that desperate if-I-can't-have-them-nobody-can state after the victim sought police intervention.

Anger blistered in her eyes. "You think I haven't considered that option, that I don't spend my days looking over my shoulder or my nights lying awake listening for sounds? I spent last night in a damn rocking chair within reach of the phone!" Silvery tears spilled onto her cheeks.

Luke brushed them away with his thumbs, rimmed with guilt at pushing her. Who the hell was he to tell her what choices to make with the terror she'd been living with? He hadn't even told her who he was and his genuine purpose for being here...but he promised himself that he'd help her and her daughter out of the situation they were in. "Okay, no police," he agreed. "But we aren't going to sit around waiting for something to happen, either. Do you have a picture of your ex-husband? Maybe I'll see a resemblance between him and the man I saw driving the green car."

"No, I left all that behind me."

"What's his name?"

Her hazel eyes were round, wary. "Rob Barrie."

Luke stared down at her, the name a gift of trust he could only equal with a display of his own feelings. He wanted so much to believe her. Wanted so much for there to be the possibility of something more between them. "Barrie, huh?" He ran his fingers lightly over her face, familiarizing himself with her fine-boned features. "I guess Calder's your maiden name." Her skin felt like damp velvet.

He wanted to kiss her, but first he needed to hear her name from her lips.

Time stilled. He could feel a tremor ripple over her face. Her lids lowered, shielding her eyes as her cheek turned into his hand as if seeking more of his touch. "Mmm-hmm. Kiss me, Luke."

His body tingled to life at her invitation. Though his police training told him he shouldn't get emotionally involved with her—not until he'd thoroughly checked out her story—the anticipation had exploded in him like a shaft of sunlight bursting through a bank of clouds. He lowered his mouth to hers, unable to hold back a moment longer.

Mary was temptation and sweetness rolled into one. And it had been so long since he'd wanted to kiss a woman. Luke fully intended the kiss to be experimental, but as she sighed with pleasure at the first brushing of his lips over hers, he claimed her mouth and found a welcome that sent his senses tumbling out of control.

He teased and caressed and explored the honeyed recesses of her mouth, suddenly consumed by an overpowering need to know her as intimately as he knew his own soul. She met his kisses with fiery-sweet hunger. He ceased to care what mission had brought him to her door. All he knew was the kiss became something more intoxicating, fueled by a torrent of emotions that had been warring inside him since the moment he'd met her. Mary slid her hands up over his chest and linked her fingers behind his neck, urging him closer.

Luke groaned, pulling her against him, thigh to thigh, hip to hip, chest to chest, letting her feel the hardness of his pulsing need. And he needed her. This Mary. Undeniably.

With trembling hands he cupped her breasts, feeling them respond to his touch though the thin layer of cotton gingham and the material of her bra as he learned their shape with his fingers, then teased the nipples into hard beads. He lowered his mouth to her breast to suckle one of those tight beads, the warm moisture and texture of cotton arousing him more painfully.

"Oh, Luke!" Mary breathed, arching her head back to improve his access, her hands greedily pulling him closer.

Luke devoted himself to the other breast, cursing and blessing the short gingham sheath she wore. While it foiled his desire to touch her breasts fully, it offered no barricade to his hands slipping beneath the narrow ruffled hem to explore the sinful sleekness of satin panties and silken buttocks...the damp heat of her beckoning him with a power he couldn't resist.

"Exquisite" was the only word Shannon could think of to describe the sensation of Luke's strong sure fingers as he touched her in the most intimate way imaginable. One hand possessed her breast, caressing, kneading. The other transgressed the elastic band of her panties, stroking and probing, while he seduced her with hot thorough kisses that made her moan incoherent words about wanting and needing and feeling. Tension mounted in her, fragile and quivering like a butterfly's wings. She arched her back, tilting her hips toward him, wanting to stay trapped in this moment forever. Luke's hand moved subtly, finding a new ultrasensitive spot that made her buck against him. Whatever he was doing...he was doing so well... The lovemaking she and Rob had so briefly shared had been pleasant, exciting, but nothing that could compare to the wild need that raced through her at breakneck speed now. Shannon broke from the powerful seduction of Luke's kiss and clutched his shoulders, gasping for breath as the spasms shuddering through her body reached a rapturous climax.

She collapsed against him, her legs limp and trembling. "Oh, my God, what was that?"

"The beginning, I hope." Luke chuckled, his gray-blue eyes glinting with obvious amusement. Shannon wasn't sure whether he was referring to sex or a more permanent relationship, neither of which she was in a position to give. He cupped her buttocks, pressing her firmly against the hard ridge outlined by his jeans. Her body instinctively shaped to fit his, testing, measuring. *I love him,* Shannon thought with a small start, wanting beyond all logic to finish what Luke's kiss had started, but the thin leafy veils of the willow tree wouldn't allow that kind of privacy.

She ran her fingers along the abrasive stubble skimming his jaw, bitterly regretting that her feelings for him would be another secret she'd have to keep, along with her name. Daring to dream of any kind of beginning with Luke seemed like tempting fate.

The old fears stole through her body, sucking up the traces of wonderment that she'd gloried in only moments before. She edged back a step, her legs pliant as modeling clay, putting distance between herself and the sensual temptation of Luke's body. She raked her fingers through her disheveled hair. "Oh, Luke. That shouldn't have happened—not with the state my life is in. It's not fair to you or me, or Samantha. Once upon a time all I wanted was to be happy. Have a family with a man I loved. Now all my dreams are about being safe and raising my daughter."

Luke felt his chest grow tight. He knew the kind of dreams Mary was talking about. The ones that filled you with hope about simple things, such as seeing his wife hold his child in her arms. Teaching that child how to ice-skate on the Rideau Canal, ride a bike, hit a baseball or roast hot dogs over a campfire. The ordinary events of a family enjoying life to the fullest. Now his dreams, like hers, were reduced to survival. But just for a minute, when he'd held Mary in his arms, when he'd kissed her, he'd felt that all those dreams were possible again.

But she was right. There was wisdom in exercising caution, taking things one step at a time. First he had to verify the facts of the story Mary had just told him. Then find out who was tormenting her here in Blossom Valley. Then maybe…

"Okay," he breathed, disciplining himself to keep his gaze off the narrow ruffle riding high across Mary's thighs as she smoothed her dress back into place. "I'm in complete agreement about keeping you and Samantha safe. How about we check out that tire together?"

Chapter Eight

Would she run now?

Luke insisted on tailing Mary home from the garage, half-convinced she was planning on running now that the mechanic had confirmed the tire had been slit.

Gut instinct told him he had better move quickly. He'd told Mary as they left the garage that she could expect him to stay as a guest on her couch until they figured out what was going on, but his adamant suggestion had not been warmly received.

He parked his car in the rutted driveway beside Abner's cottage, checking his watch as he ran inside to grab a few personal belongings. He needed to call Vaughn in Ottawa. If he was lucky, he'd catch the homicide detective before he finished his shift for the day. He wanted verification of Rob Barrie's criminal record immediately. He punched Vaughn's number into his cell phone. Fortunately the homicide detective was still at his desk.

Luke briefed him on the details of the breaking and entering, and the stolen car that had been following him. Then he quickly recounted Mary's tormented history with her ex.

"Christ, that's evil," Vaughn muttered. "Let's run his name through the system and see if the bastard exists." Luke heard the faint tapping of computer keys as Vaughn accessed the information on the Canadian Police Information Centre.

"Got him," Vaughn said. "Looks pretty much like you just told me. Got a suspended sentence—three years' probation—for the assault. And I see he's not supposed to have any contact with a Shannon Mulligan. He did some time inside for the stalking and the violation of probation convictions."

Luke's soul plummeted to the depths of hell. Mary/Shannon, whoever she was, was still lying to him. She'd left out a key detail of her story—how she'd picked up an alias—particularly *that* alias.

"Hey, Calder," Vaughn's voice barked over the line. "You still with me?"

"Yeah." Luke jerked his mind away from the leaden disappointment filling him.

"Good. Because Barrie's probation expires next Wednesday, along with the No Communications Order. How's that for a coincidence?"

"I don't believe in coincidences," Luke muttered. "He sounds like the type to bide his time, waiting for his probation to end so he can legally approach her."

"I'll get copies of the police reports for Barrie's arrests and track down his probation officer. See if he can tell me Barrie's current whereabouts."

"Can you get me a photo of Shannon Mulligan so I can positively ID her? And Barrie's mug shot? I want to know whether he was the one driving the stolen car."

"Give me a day or two, and you can pick them up at the RCMP detachment. If the suspect turns out to be Shannon Mulligan, I'll contact the security department of the Blossom Valley Bank about her attempt to defraud them. They'll be relieved they denied her the loan, but they'll want to charge her with Personation with Intent."

Luke knew charges would have to be brought against her, but that didn't make the thought of such a happening any more bearable. "Do me a favor. When you check in with Barrie's probation officer, ask him to find out where Barrie was on St. Patrick's Day last year."

"Where you going with this, Calder?"

"Hell, I don't know. But this woman's a dead ringer for my wife. Maybe Barrie thought so, too."

IT WAS A GUT-TWISTING form of torture to be under the same roof with Mary with the suspicions that festered in Luke's mind. Suspicions that wouldn't be confirmed until he saw a picture of Shannon Mulligan. At least Mary had changed out of the short gingham dress she'd been wearing earlier into a less-revealing pair of beige twill shorts and a pale leaf-green top, for which Luke was grateful. He wanted no reminders of how he'd betrayed the memory of his wife this afternoon by desiring this woman.

And yet even while he harbored such thoughts, he noted the soft swell of her breasts rising below the scoop neck of her top as she bent over to lift Samantha out of her high chair after supper. He remembered unwillingly how Mary's skin had felt beneath his palms, how she'd tasted, how she'd responded to his touch. Remembered how he'd wanted to peel off that dress and make love to her behind the sheltering curtain of willow branches.

He still wanted her. How could something that had felt so miraculous be wrong?

Luke schooled himself to be civil, to keep the dark thoughts thrashing in his brain from tainting his conversation with bitterness. There was already enough tension in the room. Mary's reluctance to have him sleeping on her couch was palpable. But with careful handling, she might still provide a viable lead in his wife's murder.

He picked the plates off the counter and put them in the sink, then filled the sink with hot water and dish detergent. From the bathroom he heard the sounds of splashing, Samantha's goslinglike squawks and the murmur of Mary's voice drifting in the still air of the summer evening. Peaceful contented sounds that left him feeling like some malevolent marauder who'd come to swoop down and destroy this happy home Mary had built with her daughter.

Finishing the dishes, he went out to sit on the front steps, scanning the vegetation for signs of a Peeping Tom or stalker as the sun slowly made its descent toward the golden hills circling Kettle Lake.

Twenty minutes later he heard Mary's footsteps as she approached the screen door. He turned his head, seeing her behind the fine mesh of the screen, examining her body language. Hesitation was clearly etched in the worry lines framing her mouth.

"Samantha's in bed. Everything okay out there?"

"Seems to be," he said curtly, then reminded himself to be civil. "Thought I'd sit out here awhile," he added with a drawl of dry amusement. "Let him get a good long look at me."

Shannon bit hard on her lower lip, affronted and angry that even in the twenty-first century this type of caveman mentality was still going strong. Luke was sprawled in a casual position on her front steps—elbows propped on the step behind him, shoulder muscles bunched, brown hair slightly ruffled as if he'd just run his fingers through it, and his long legs spread out in territorial fashion in front of him. "You think Dylan or Rob or whoever is out there will back off because there's two hundred pounds of testosterone plunked on my front steps?"

"Hundred and eighty-five pounds," he corrected mildly. "As much as I'm sure this insults your feminist principles, bad guys, be they male or female, select victims who appear vulnerable and seem to be easy targets. You're a woman living alone with a baby in a fairly isolated spot. I'm just letting whoever is out there know that you're not alone and that you're no longer an easy target. If he happens to notice I can beat the crap out of him, so much the better."

Alarm jangled through her at the thought of Luke throwing a punch at anyone. This was a side of him she had not seen, a sharp contrast to the calming gentleness that inhabited his eyes and his hands. But then, she knew she'd fight like a wildcat if anyone posed a physical threat to her baby. Kill, if she had to. Still, she wasn't about to admit that Luke was right. "What makes you such an expert on criminals?" she said waspishly through the screen, determined to keep some kind of physical barrier between them.

Luke laughed roughly. "I used to be a teenager. It's a jungle out there." He lazily shifted his legs, crossing his ankles as if he meant to stay there permanently. And not just on her steps or on her couch.

In her bed.

Where she wanted him, if she was honest with herself. Her body still pulsated with suppressed desire to finish what had been ignited between them this afternoon. To touch him as intimately as he had touched her, experience the wonder of being lost in his kiss and feel the thrust of his hips as his body joined with hers. Ask him what he'd done as a teenager that made him think the world was a jungle. But she'd forfeited all rights to honesty. Her eyes grazed hungrily over his dark head and broad shoulders, soaking in the memory of how close he'd brought her to heaven this afternoon. Without another word she stepped away from the door, leaving Luke to continue with his sentry duty. She'd made her bed when she'd assumed Mary Calder's identity. And she'd lie in it—alone.

THE PORCH LIGHT was off, and the night-vision scope revealed the green shape of the man sprawled on the front steps of the cottage like a faithful mutt protecting its master. Did he think he could protect her from him? He'd learn soon enough. Everything was in place and the slut would soon get what was coming to her. He had all the time in the world to watch and wait for his prey to appear. Then he'd get away with murder.

LUKE ENDURED the weekend under Mary's roof, lying awake at night listening to the rustling of her blankets as she shifted restlessly. Wondering all the while as his body coiled with tension if she was awake, thinking up new lies to spin.

Shannon Mulligan hadn't picked Mary Tatiana Calder's name and birth date at random—or even from Mary's obituary in the paper, because Luke hadn't given the paper his wife's birth date or her middle name.

Which presented the burning question—how had she come by the information? Had she bought his wife's identity from a scumbag on the street? Or had she somehow known his wife or been involved with her murder?

The days were easier than the nights because he could secrete himself in the workshop with his thoughts and the power tools, the baby monitor turned on for safety reasons so that he could hear if Mary was suddenly in trouble in the cottage.

Of course, it also meant that he could hear every loving word she said to Samantha. Hear the songs she sung. Hear the sounds of their life together—toys tumbling to the floor, the creak of the rocking chair, the gurgle of the coffeemaker and the sucking noise Samantha made when she took her bottle.

Midmorning Monday as he traced, cut and sanded the human-shaped forms for Mary's garden guardians—folksy painted characters from varying walks of life sporting miniature straw hats, gardening gloves and neighborly smiles—the blunt edge of doubt burrowed under his skin. When would Vaughn send the photos of Shannon Mulligan and Robert Barrie? Today? Tomorrow? He couldn't stand the waiting much longer.

As if in response to his silent entreaties, his cell phone vibrated in the pocket of his jeans. Luke abandoned the piece he was sanding by hand, tugged off his dust mask and dug the phone out of his pocket. The sound of water running in the sink over the intercom—probably Mary rinsing out her coffee cup—reassured him that he could take the call without risk of blowing his cover.

Luke's heart clenched like a fist when Staff Sergeant Rayford identified himself and advised him that some photos had arrived for Luke at the RCMP detachment. Unwilling to leave Mary without protection, Luke asked if an unmarked car and plainclothes officer were available to deliver it to him. Rayford agreed and arrangements were made to have it delivered within the hour.

Luke met the plainclothes officer, a petite brunette with a no-nonsense expression, at the appointed spot along the path and took possession of the envelope. He concealed it underneath his T-shirt until he was back in the workshop. Over the intercom, he could hear Mary opening cupboards in the kitchen, offering Samantha a teething biscuit. She hadn't missed him.

Dust-covered fingers trembling, he tore open the envelope. Two sheets of paper slid onto the workbench. Anguish caught in his throat as he stared at the color copy of Shannon Mulligan's Nova Scotia driver's-license photo. The hair was different. But the rest…there was no mistaking the eyes or the mouth or those cheeks. Shannon Mulligan was the name of the woman who'd hired him, who'd been lying to him for the past week.

It shouldn't hurt, shouldn't even matter to him, but it did.

Luke drew a deep shuddering breath of cedar and sawdust-tainted air and looked at the mug shots of Robert Barrie, studying the frontal and profile shots of the intense-looking dark-haired man for some hint of recognition. None came.

This was not the driver of the green car that had been tailing them, Luke was certain of it. Just as he was certain that he'd seen the person who'd been following them before. He still couldn't place him.

Was the driver someone local Robert Barrie had hired? Or someone connected to Donna White—a boyfriend, acquaintance or other relative whom Dylan had roped into helping him? Or maybe it was the other way around, and a boyfriend or other relative had enlisted the teenager's help?

Luke punched in Vaughn's number. The phone rang several times before the detective's voicemail kicked in. Luke left a terse message, bound by duty to his wife and duty to the badge he wore. "It's her."

Events were slipping out of his control. Maybe the judge would be lenient with her.

SOMETHING WAS WRONG. Shannon could sense it as she watched Luke woodenly chewing his supper.

"You're awfully quiet," she remarked as she spooned applesauce into Samantha's mouth, dribbling some onto her daughter's chin. "Is there something you're not telling me? Have you seen someone?"

The air of watchfulness that visibly slipped over his face, shutting her out, brought a warning chill to her heart. "No, I haven't seen hide nor hair of anyone in the last few days, though I thought I'd walk down to the beach after supper to see if Dylan's selling ice cream. What about you? Is there something you're not telling me?" he returned quietly, his gray-blue eyes strangely solemn.

Oh, God, he knows! Shannon thought, taken aback. But how could he...? She floundered for a second, then realized sadly that her revelation that her ex-husband was still alive had obviously ruptured the lines of trust between them. Or maybe he intuited that she was still holding something back. She'd be flattered that he knew her so well if it didn't hurt so much knowing that nothing could come of a relationship between them. "No, nothing's happened. No wrong numbers, visitors or Peeping Toms. You would have heard them over the intercom, anyway." He didn't look appeased by her statement.

Was it possible he was just tired from sleeping on her couch? For a man of his height, it probably wasn't very comfortable. And for all she knew, he was probably lying awake all night listening for intruders. "You don't have to sleep on the couch, you know—" She broke off, coloring at how that must have sounded like an invitation. "I meant, we could alternate taking the bed or the couch. Take turns taking watch."

Luke stood up abruptly. "I'm fine on the couch," he said tersely, putting an end to the discussion. He gathered his dishes, setting them in the sink with a clatter. "I'm heading down to the beach now. I want to see what Dylan does when he finishes his rounds. Don't worry, I'll be nearby. Lock the door behind me.''

Before she could so much as say a word, he was out the door, running.

DON'T HANG UP. Luke yanked the cell phone from his pocket the second he hit cover, hoping that the insistent vibrations meant that Vaughn was returning his call. ''Calder here.''

''About time, Calder!'' Vaughn's voice scraped over the line. ''Listen, I got your message, but before we get into that topic, something creepy is going on down here. Someone's nosing around asking questions about you. Making discreet inquiries.''

Luke felt the muscles in his back tingle as he scanned the nearby tree trunks and shrubs for possible threats. Sunset was a good two hours away, yet he felt a lengthening shadow being cast over him. ''What the hell are you implying, Vaughn?''

''I'm saying that I don't think it's a concerned buddy wondering about the state of your health.''

Luke's mind reeled. ''Could it be Barrie? Maybe he's got some connections we don't know about? The guy organizes conferences. Maybe he did one with a police agency.''

''Your guess is as good as mine. But his probation officer can't get hold of him. He talked to his landlord, who said Barrie went away on a business trip, but Barrie didn't advise his probation officer of the trip. And get this—apparently Barrie was in Montreal scouting out conference sites on St. Patrick's Day last year. Didn't you tell me that Shannon Mulligan told you she'd changed jobs and moved several times, even out of province in order to get away from her ex? Maybe she moved to Ottawa and Barrie followed.''

Luke felt sweat bead on his brow and trickle down his temples. Montreal was a two-hour-and-fifteen-minute drive from Ottawa. Close enough that it fell within the realm of possibility that Barrie could be placed at Mary Calder's murder scene. "So maybe Barrie mistook Mary for Shannon and attacked her in her car?'' Luke quickly rejected the idea even as he voiced it. "No, that doesn't fit. Shannon had personal information about Mary that wasn't readily available. Her birth date. Especially her middle name.''

"What if your wife offered Shannon Mulligan a ride and Shannon was in the car when the attack occurred? Could have been a random attack. She grabbed Mary's purse and ran.''

"If it was a random attack, I think Shannon would have called for an ambulance—even if she'd stolen the purse. But if it was her ex, maybe not. Testifying against him in court would mean he'd discover that she was pregnant.''

"But he'd no longer be a threat if he was serving time for murder—''

"*If* he was convicted. I don't think she has that much faith in the judicial process.'' Luke massaged his forehead. This was moving like a fast-forwarded video, and Luke couldn't grasp all the images and make sense of the plot. "Even so, I didn't recognize Barrie from the mug shots. He wasn't our tail.''

"So maybe Barrie hired a local thug from Ottawa, which would explain why the guy looked familiar.''

Another possibility leaped into Luke's mind as he realized Shannon's tire had been slit *after* he'd arrived in British Columbia. Had someone followed him here? Someone who thought his wife was still alive and had survived her attack?

Luke hesitated, thinking the theory through as he shared it with Vaughn. "Maybe the tail looked familiar to me because it was someone I met through my wife. She was in public relations and dragged me to all kinds of social, business and political events. Whoever has been making inquiries about me has to have some powerful connections—"

Vaughn swore. "You got a motive to go with that theory, Constable?" Luke knew the detective's deliberate use of his rank was a sharp rap on his knuckles to remind him that Vaughn was calling the shots.

Luke kept pushing. Vaughn wouldn't have warned him about those discreet inquiries if the detective wasn't worried there was more to Mary's murder than a failed carjacking attempt. "Not yet, but there might be one that we've overlooked. Maybe she happened upon some information that an influential person didn't want to be made public. I know you made copies of my wife's day planner at the early stages of her murder investigation. Can you fax me copies of it? Maybe looking at it will trigger something."

Vaughn's voice had a decided strain to it. "I'll contact Staff Sergeant Rayford and do it immediately. And advise him of the situation. You might need to call in reinforcements."

Luke hated to ask, but he needed to know. "What

about the bank? Will they be pressing charges against Shannon Mulligan?''

"Haven't had a chance to notify them—I've been out working another homicide. I'm calling in someone from the fraud division to assist. We want to move carefully. Pressing charges too soon may prevent us from catching a bigger fish. If you're right and your wife's killer has followed you to British Columbia on the assumption that your wife is still alive, it would not be strategic on our part to place her under arrest and alert the killer to the fact that she's an imposter.''

Luke gritted his teeth. "You're willing to use her as bait?'' His tone must have conveyed his personal feelings on the matter.

"You're with her twenty-four–seven, Calder. She's got better protection than the speaker of the House. Besides, if it turns out she's involved in something bigger than impersonation, she might be persuaded to talk in exchange for the lesser charge. So hold tight.''

Yeah, hold tight, without so much as a sidearm to protect Shannon and Samantha from a killer who might be stalking them. Luke sighed and turned off the phone.

Every muscle in his body was screaming for physical release. He stalked off down the path to the beach.

From a distance he saw Dylan White manning his ice-cream cart, the surly curl to his lip visible as he served a circle of customers.

Luke found a hiding spot behind a tree and waited for the teen to finish. It would be dark soon. Where did Dylan go when he went off duty?

Chapter Nine

A chilly smile pulled at Luke's mouth as Dylan abandoned the ice-cream cart in a thick clump of bushes. Veering off the path, the teenager threaded through the trees toward Shannon's cottage.

Luke followed him at a discreet distance, wondering what kind of malicious mischief the boy had on his mind tonight. Reaching the perimeter of Shannon's property, Dylan circled around, dodging from tree trunk to tree trunk, his unnaturally bleached hair gleaming like a ghostly aura.

Suddenly he slipped through a crease between two shrubs and disappeared into their depths. The sound of crackling branches indicated the teen was climbing a nearby tree. Luke moved to a better position, noting that Dylan's elevated location gave him an unobstructed view deep into Shannon's kitchen. There were no curtains on that window, only a swath of bright fabric looped along a rod. The light in the kitchen was on, and Luke saw Shannon appear at the sink, probably preparing Samantha's bedtime bottle.

Luke observed and listened, attuning himself to every sound and smell in the vicinity. The sounds of insects hummed in the air, as one with the evening as the lingering scent of barbecued hot dogs and steaks.

He moved closer to the tree where Dylan was concealed.

"Mind if I ask what you're doing up there?" he growled in a don't-give-me-any-crap-tough-guy tone.

A muffled reply, couched with bravado, drifted down. "Watchin' the stars."

"What, you think I'm stupid? I've been watching you, Dylan. I know what you've been doing. I know about the phone calls. You're heading into some serious trouble—and let me tell you that wasting your life locked up in a room the size of a bathroom is something you should avoid. You don't even get to crap in private."

"I haven't done anything!"

"And neither has that lady you've been terrorizing. She's working herself ragged to run a business and support her baby—only very strange things keep happening to her, and I think we both know why."

"You don't know what the hell you're talking about."

"Are you denying that you threw a couple of rocks at Mary and her baby last week? You're lucky you didn't kill them."

"I didn't throw rocks at anybody!"

"Dylan, you're not going to solve your mother's problems by getting arrested. You'll only compound them. Now I'm going to do you a favor and forget that I've seen you here or that I noticed that none of your mother's crafts were damaged in the break-in at Glorie's Gifts Galore."

"What?"

That got his attention.

Luke went on mercilessly now that the boy was listening. "Yeah, and if I can figure it out, I'm sure the RCMP will, too, especially if they were to find out about your nighttime tree-climbing habit. I'm sure they can trace the phone calls you made. I wonder how many ice-cream bars you'd have to sell to repay Glorie for the damages to her store? Maybe you ought to think about it before you come down from that tree. While you're at it, think about how you're going to make something of yourself to do your mother proud. Oh, and one more thing. If I catch you around here again or find out you've been up to your old tricks, you'll be seeing stars. And they won't be the sky variety."

Figuring he'd made his point, Luke strode off into the darkness.

DYLAN CLUNG to the rough sap-sticky branch as the hot sting of urine trickled down his leg. Who the hell was that, accusing him of trying to kill somebody? He'd never throw a rock at anyone, especially a baby. So what if he'd called Mary Calder once or twice just to bug her. It wasn't like he'd threatened her or anything. He just hated her and wished she'd go back to wherever she came from so his life would return to the way it used to be. Since the stores had started cutting back on their orders, his mom spent her days in tears, rarely changing out of her tattered bathrobe, working on new stuff that didn't sell any better than her old stuff. Which only made her cry more and made him feel helpless and angry. What was he going to do now? The stuff the man had said about Glorie's Gifts Galore was reason enough for Dylan to be seriously worried.

SHANNON GAVE a guilty start when she heard the tap on the door. Luke was back! She quickly zipped the duffel bag she'd been stuffing with clothes and slid it under her bed. She'd packed enough clothes and diapers that she and Samantha could get by for a week. Her emergency stash of cash was tucked in her purse. All she needed to do now was find a way to get Samantha into the truck and slip away without Luke's noticing. He was too close to knowing all her secrets, and she couldn't draw him knowingly or unknowingly into the fraud she was perpetrating. She cared about him too much to involve him as a conspirator. And the thought of him calling her Mary as he made love to her was unbearable. And no matter how much she tried to resist it, she knew that sooner or later they would make love. The tension straining between them was like a cord stretched to its limit. Inevitably it would fray strand by strand until it broke.

"Mary?" The low murmur of Luke's voice accompanied another discreet tap on the door.

Shannon brushed her hands over her damp cheeks, nervous butterflies flitting in her stomach as she raced through the cottage that had once been her sanctuary to unlock the front door. She'd fled so many times before, what was one more?

The knowledge that this was not like all those other times imprinted on her heart as Luke stepped into the cottage, bringing the scents of the summer night with him. Shannon absorbed the heady combination of pine and sand and the dusky tang of Luke's skin. The line of his jaw had never looked as sharp as it did tonight. His gray-blue eyes bored into her with a steady determination that had the power to defeat all her defenses. For a fraction of a second, Shannon let herself entertain the foolish fantasy of loosening the top button of his jeans and having sex with him. No words. No names. Just hot frenzied sex.

Her knees began to quiver. ''What happened?'' she demanded weakly.

''I ran into Dylan. We had a talk. Or rather, I talked and he listened, as he was in a somewhat awkward position.''

''What do you mean, awkward?''

Luke's wry recounting of how he'd followed Dylan to a tree that overlooked her cottage left Shannon stunned and grappling for a stool to sit on. Luke leaned stiffly against the door frame, his arms crossed over his chest as if he was doing his utmost to maintain a respectable distance from her. ''He denied throwing the rocks at you and Samantha. He didn't comment on the phone calls, but I got a strong reaction out of him when I mentioned the burglary at Glorie's gift shop.''

''Do you believe him?''

''He was up a tree watching you through your kitchen window. The jury's still out.'' Luke turned his back to her and bolted the front door, his tone low and husky and sparking a fire of wanting in Shannon's belly. ''But maybe things aren't quite what you think.'' He cleared his throat, suddenly brisk again. ''Are you finished in the bathroom? I could use a shower.''

''Go ahead. There are fresh towels on the rod.'' Shannon stared after him, her thoughts in turmoil. Should she grab Samantha from her crib and make a run for her truck while Luke was in the shower? If Dylan was behind the pranks, she had no reason to run—except from her feelings for Luke. The water turned on in the bathroom with a drumming sound. Time was running out. She had to make a decision.

Her gaze slid to the flower-pot-shaped key rack beside the door where she saw that Luke had already made the decision for her. Her truck keys, along with the spare key, which she normally kept hanging on the brass hook beside her workshop keys, were gone. Was this his way of telling her he wanted her to stay?

CONFRONTING LUKE DIRECTLY about the keys was out of the question, Shannon decided at breakfast the next morning. She was brooding over her second cup of French vanilla coffee, while Luke examined the designs she'd made for recycling into scarecrows some old fence posts she'd purchased at a yard sale. She'd have to be more subtle. Samantha had grasped at him this morning with her grubby porridge hands, hiking up his black hockey T-shirt to reveal a suspicious-looking bulge in the right front pocket of his jeans. Shannon had a feeling those were her keys. Maybe she could suggest they go to the grocery store for milk and diapers. Or she could make an excuse to go to the bank. She could get her hands on the keys and draw out more cash from her account to add to her emergency stash.

Darn him, anyway, for knowing her better than she knew herself. Was she really that transparent?

His eyes were warm, appreciative, softening the hard line of his mouth when he glanced up from her sketches. "This is a clever design, especially the way the arms are attached with screws so they can be moved. Gives them character. Is this what you'd like me to get started on today?"

She shouldn't let it, but his praise buoyed her. Rob had always belittled her efforts, chipping away at her confidence. Possibly Luke was trying to distract her with work so she wouldn't spend the day fretting and worrying if the phone calls and pranks would cease now that he'd confronted Dylan. He'd obviously adopted a wait-and-see attitude for himself. Still, whatever his objective, his praise meant something to her. "That's the plan," she said, matching his effort to be positive. "I've got some leftover ends of two-by-eights in the scrap box for the bases. And some one-by-three scraps will do for the arm pieces. I'm not sure of the precise length. We'll start with one as a model and refine it."

"Sounds like fun."

Despite the part of her that felt pushed to the wall to escape her attraction to him, Shannon responded to his enthusiasm for the project, her creative spirit exulting in the prospect of spending the morning in the workshop with him, sharing ideas. To hide her discomfiture, she dispatched him to the workshop to hunt through the scrap box while she finished up the dishes.

Her heart beat double time in syncopation with his footsteps as he sauntered across the room. Out of the corner of her eye, she tracked his movements as he lifted the workshop key off the key rack on his way out the door.

Of course, he didn't say one word about the missing truck keys.

LUKE WAS CONSCIOUSLY aware of the minutes passing as he left the cottage and walked out to the workshop. Rayford had phoned last night, necessitating Luke's hasty retreat to the bathroom to shower, and they'd arranged a drop for this morning. Vaughn had faxed the pages of Mary's day planner.

It had rained during the night, leaving the ground slightly damp and the sky freshly cleansed. Small white clouds dotted the blue sky like popped corn. Luke unlocked the workshop and flicked on the fluorescent light. Then with a quick glance over his shoulder to make sure Shannon wasn't watching him from the cottage, he slipped outside into the trees behind the garage. The same female officer who'd made yesterday's delivery was strolling along the needle-strewn path, a straw tote in one hand as if she was headed to the beach.

"Rayford's keeping a car in the area if you need assistance," the constable told him, discreetly passing him a manila envelope.

Yet another reason to keep his emotions out of the situation, Luke reminded himself as he slid the envelope under his shirt and returned to the workshop. He managed to hide it behind the cabinet where he'd concealed yesterday's photos before Shannon arrived with Samantha in one arm and a portable playpen in the other. A bag of toys was slung over her shoulder. His examination of the pages of his wife's day planner would have to wait until Shannon left him alone in the workshop.

He unburdened Shannon of the playpen, setting it up in the shade. But one look at Shannon's backside as she bent over to settle Samantha in the playpen sent him recoiling into the workshop, his fingers curling tightly around the scrap lumber he should be sorting. *It's not personal. The law's the law,* he told himself as Shannon joined him in the workshop, bringing the exotic scent of jasmine into the confined space. But whatever she'd done had affected him personally. Now he only wanted it to be over and done with so he could retreat to his condo and never have to think about the feelings she'd resurrected in him. Even now, his body betrayed everything he believed in—he wanted her.

By lunchtime, Luke was hot, sweaty and still painfully aroused. Through trial and error, they had cut and assembled two post scarecrows—because Shannon had decided halfway through the process that she should do a female version as a mate to her original male design. Each stood four feet tall on a two-inch-thick base, arms attached to the sides at shoulder height with screws. Shannon would paint on faces and clothes, and finish them off with raffia hair, straw hats and bandannas. They'd be hot sellers.

Luke was relieved when Samantha grew bored with her toys and demanded her mother's attention. Shannon's disappearance into the cottage with Samantha gave him a temporary respite from the sexual and emotional tug-of-war of being in her presence.

Luke carried the scarecrows up to the small front porch, where Shannon planned to paint them this afternoon while Samantha napped.

They had lunch outside at the round picnic table. Samantha was rubbing her eyes with her fists, her head drooping onto the high chair's tray before the meal was over. Luke gently lifted the infant's silky dark head so Shannon could slide back the tray and release Samantha from the straps.

Samantha molded herself to her mother's breast, burrowing her head into the curve of Shannon's shoulder. Luke watched them go into the cottage with something akin to regret. But what would happen to Samantha if her mother was arrested wasn't his concern.

Luke carried the cups and plates into the cottage and hurried back to the workshop. Knowing his time was limited, he made short work of cutting the bases and bodies for a half-dozen scarecrows. The arms could wait until after he'd looked at the contents of the envelope Vaughn had sent.

Luke eased open the workshop door to check on Shannon. She was occupied on the porch with her scarecrows, bottles of paint aligned like soldiers on the narrow porch railing beside her ever-present coffee mug.

He could count on some privacy for a little while at least. Samantha usually napped for a couple of hours. Luke opened the envelope. The sight of his wife's handwriting, even though it was dehumanized by the process of photocopying, brought a rush of memories. The last precious months they'd spent together replayed in his mind, followed by the agonizing shock and grief of her murder and the frustration of a police investigation that was going nowhere. He started with the January entries, the entry on the first day of the year stopping him cold. "Make a baby."

The words on the page swam before his eyes as he struggled to get a grip on himself.

He could do this. *Please, God, give me the strength to do this with dispassion.*

Hands shaking, he ripped several sheets of paper toweling from the holder on the wall and used a carpenter's pencil to make notes. He planned to list the names of everyone his wife had dealt with in the few months before her death, including the names of people he remembered meeting at the functions he'd attended with his wife. He'd worked his way through the first week and a half of January when it occurred to him that pictures of the functions and guest lists might be available. And he knew who might be able to supply him with both.

Fortunately his wife's former secretary, Erin Flynn, a paragon of efficiency with a heart of gold who'd moved on to work for another PR firm after his wife's death, responded to his telephoned request with a steadfast, "Consider it done, Luke."

He read her the list of functions and the dates and welcomed her offer to include a guest list and photos of the St. Patrick's Day party at the country club where Mary had stopped to consult with a client about a press release the night she'd died. Erin also promised to dig up whatever photos she could of Ottawa's movers and shakers. The wider net he threw, the greater chance he might prod his memory into recalling why the driver of that green car had seemed so familiar.

PAINTING HAD ALWAYS BEEN an outlet for the stress bottling up in Shannon. Today was no different. She could feel the tension flow out her hand and dissipate with every stroke of her brush. The repetitive motion had a calming effect on her thoughts about the man who'd commandeered her heart and her truck keys.

With the sun warming her head and shoulders and the scarecrows' personalities emerging at her fingertips, it was easier to center herself. Find the simple truths that eluded her when she was overwhelmed with fear. And now the truths hit her, painful as Rob's blows had been. All the rationalizations in the world couldn't sugarcoat the truth that she didn't like the woman she'd become. She was ashamed of herself for hoping, simply because it was the lesser of two evils, that another woman's child had resorted to playing pranks on her as a twisted way of dealing with his mother's financial problems. And ashamed that in her zeal to protect her daughter, she'd lost herself.

Not just her name. But her principles and her family…and her innermost desires. She didn't want Luke to leave. The morning spent in the workshop with him, though spiked with bittersweet tension, had confirmed that to her in a multitude of unspoken ways. His hands were at home on her tools and at ease caring for her daughter. When Samantha had fussed because she'd thrown a toy out of her playpen, Luke had scooped up the toy and proceeded to play a game with her. He'd even picked her up and held her in the crook of his arm, giving her a bottle of juice while Shannon had drawn and redrawn the lines of the arms on a block of wood, trying to get the design just right.

And all the while he'd looked at her with unspoken questions in his eyes. She just wanted to be worthy of the woman Luke saw when he looked at her with barely checked desire darkening his gaze. Shannon dropped her paintbrush in a jar of water and examined the engaging expressions the male and female scarecrows wore, laughter sparking in their bright green eyes as if they knew the secret to happiness. Was it too late to find her way back to that woman?

A crow passing overhead jeered at her wishful thinking. Some of her mistakes couldn't be erased. And Rob, well, the threat he posed was like a land mine primed to explode at her first misstep. She'd never forgive herself if Rob ever found out he had a daughter.

Shannon checked her watch, surprised by the lateness of the hour. Samantha had been napping almost three hours. Being in the fresh air this morning must have tired her out. That and the heat of the afternoon.

Shannon stepped gratefully into the cooler temperatures of the cottage. It was too hot to think about refilling her coffee cup. She'd make a pitcher of iced tea and bring a glass out to Luke after she woke Samantha.

She washed her brushes at the sink, ears cocked for sounds that her daughter was awake and babbling contentedly to herself. She always woke in a sunny mood.

There were no noises. Shannon eased open the door. "Hello, sleepyhead…"

In the two seconds it took to register the sliced window screen and the empty crib, the bottom dropped out of her world. Samantha was gone!

Chapter Ten

Luke was so completely absorbed in the exercise that he didn't hear Shannon's approach until it was too late.

The door to the workshop jerked open. Sunlight flooded into the workshop, framing Shannon in the doorway. Luke instinctively moved to block her view of the workbench where he'd spread out the pages of his wife's day planner. But the white coat of fear on her features told him it was too late.

Her voice was wafer-thin with despair. "Samantha's not in her crib. Someone cut her window screen and took her." Luke forgot about the incriminating papers as Shannon thrust a sheet of white paper at him, her hand shaking violently. It was a note composed in blood-red lipstick warning her not to call the police or she would never see her baby alive again. Horror dawning, Luke read the words a second time.

How could someone have snatched her? He glanced at the baby monitor, then realized it wasn't on. They hadn't turned it on this morning because Samantha had been in the playpen right beside the garage and he'd been so caught up in Mary's day planner that he'd forgotten. Guilt slashed and burned through his mid-section. He was supposed to be protecting them!

Shannon gripped his arm. "I think Rob has her! Oh, God, why didn't I check on her sooner? She never sleeps more than two and a half hours." Her grip on his arm tightened, her nails biting into his skin. "This is your fault. If you hadn't taken the keys to my truck, I would have left last night!"

"And then what? You'd keep running for the rest of your life, always looking over your shoulder?" He eased his arm free of her death grip, wanting to hold her and tell her that they'd get Samantha back. But fear and the knowledge of the diminishing odds of retrieving a stolen child were pushing him into action. "Look, there's no point in arguing. We have to focus on getting Samantha safely home." He fished his cell phone out of his pocket, striding toward the door. Maybe Barrie left some kind of tracks. "We need to call the police."

Shannon lunged at him, trying to wrestle the phone out of his hand. "No! The note said he'd kill her!"

Luke tried to restrain her, fighting with her for the phone. "What do you expect? A note that says, 'Please call the police so I can be arrested as soon as possible?' He's playing with your mind. He's not likely to hurt her. If Rob stole Samantha, he probably wants to be a father to her."

Shannon elbowed him sharply in the ribs.

Luke grunted in pain and slipped his arms around her, pinning her upper arms as he pulled her against his chest. "Stop it! I don't want to hurt you. Every second you delay phoning the police puts him one second farther away from capture. You want her back, don't you?''

She sagged against him, a sob breaking from her lips. "Oh, Luke, please don't do this! If you call the police, they'll arrest me.''

Luke hesitated, breathing hard from the struggle and the fear that Rob would be long gone with Samantha. "Arrest you for what? If there's something you haven't told me, you'd better make it fast.''

"I...I've been committing fraud. My name isn't Mary Calder. It's Shannon Mulligan. I left town the day my doctor told me I was pregnant. I was in shock. I packed a bag and caught a flight to Ottawa, hoping to start over again. When I was on the plane I read an article in a magazine about identity fraud. The article described how easily stolen ID could be purchased in any city. I thought the only way to be certain Rob couldn't find me again was to completely change my identity and disappear. Once I arrived in Ottawa I checked into a hotel, then went out and did just what the article said—I asked a taxi driver to take me to an area known for solicitation, then I found a prostitute and asked her if she knew where I could buy some stolen ID. She offered me some on the spot. It cost fifty dollars.''

Luke forced out the question that had brought him here and braced himself for the answer. "Do you know who the woman is that you're impersonating?''

Shannon shook her head, her fragrant hair brushing his chin. "No. Just someone who was unfortunate to have her purse stolen. Some credit cards came with the set, but I destroyed those. Before I went back to the airport the next morning, I found a hair salon and had my hair bleached and cut to resemble Mary Calder's driver's-license photo. I bought a ticket for Vancouver using her ID. Then a bus ticket to the Okanagan. I've been in Blossom Valley ever since.''

His arm around her waist relaxed its iron hold as he weighed her words. If she hadn't read an Ottawa newspaper or seen the news during her brief overnight stay, it was plausible that she wasn't aware that the woman whose ID she'd bought had been murdered. If that was the case, she wasn't an accessory to murder. That mattered more to him personally than he cared to admit, but he'd examine those feelings if and when they got Samantha safely back.

At least her real identity was out in the open. ''Calling in the police is a risk you have to take, Shannon, if you want your daughter back. The police are trained to deal with emergencies like this. This is a huge area. They can set up roadblocks and maybe a judge will be sympathetic if you turn yourself in—''

Shannon lifted her head, her chin jutting sharply. ''I said no, Luke. I'll just have to wait for Rob to call or leave another note. He's probably going to arrange a meeting because he wants the three of us together.''

Luke rested his cheek against her temple, feeling the trembling of her slight frame. ''What if you're wrong and it isn't Rob who took her? What if it's someone else?''

She twisted around to face him, anxiety rising in her hazel eyes. ''How can you say that? It has to be Rob! I can't believe Dylan would do something like this. Are you suggesting he did this because you caught him trespassing last night?''

Luke took a deep breath. She wasn't listening and the time had come to level with her—Samantha's safety was at stake. ''Shannon, listen to me,'' he said grimly. ''I'm not a construction worker from Vancouver. I'm a cop from Ottawa. The woman whose identity you purchased was murdered. And I think her killer has tracked you here in the mistaken belief that Mary Calder is still alive.''

SHANNON SWAYED as if her body was made of flimsy paper. No, no, no, what Luke was saying couldn't be true! Her mind locked into denial mode, unwilling to accept the information Luke was forcing on her. Her precious baby might be in the hands of a killer, and she'd just confessed committing a crime to a police officer. Was he going to arrest her?

Now she saw that he'd only been saying and doing everything he could to earn her trust. ''The tire?'' she spit out, disillusioned and disheartened that she'd managed to misjudge him just as she'd foolishly misjudged Rob. And here she'd thought Luke was one of a rare breed, the kind of honorable soul-stirring man whose kisses were a fantasy come to life. Everything that had happened between them had been meaningless and had landed her in yet another nightmare. ''Did you slit it so you could worm your way into my confidence?''

''I didn't have anything to do with it. I'd been conducting surveillance on you that morning. I saw you make your deliveries and followed you into the hardware store. That's where I read your ad for a woodworker. Unfortunately I didn't see anyone put that rattle on your truck or slit your tire.''

"But you had references!''

He shrugged. ''Buddies in the brotherhood from Vancouver.''

Shannon assumed he meant the police brotherhood. "How did the police find me?''

"A tip from the credit bureau. Something about a bank loan you applied for.''

Shannon swallowed hard. The house of cards she'd built for herself was falling down around her. She couldn't lose her baby along with everything else! She had to know more details. She forced herself to think. "How did Mary Calder die?''

Luke's eyes narrowed on her like glittering glass beads. ''It was made to look like an attempted carjacking. She was beaten to death and her purse was stolen. We think she recognized her killer. Someone's been snooping into her murder case in Ottawa.''

"Oh, my God. And you think that person is after me now? But why take my baby?''

"I don't have all the answers, Shannon. But Samantha's abduction is serious enough that it's imperative we pool every piece of information we've got. What day did you buy Mary Calder's ID?''

"St. Patrick's Day.''

"What time?''

"I'm not sure—maybe 11:30 or 11:45 p.m. I was very nervous. I got back to the hotel just after midnight.''

"Can you describe the prostitute who sold it to you?''

"She was older—late thirties or early forties. Lots of makeup. Blond hair. Flamboyant, but very jittery, like she was on drugs or something. She was wearing a cheap white fur cape over a black dress with sequins and peek-a-boo slits, and black leather boots with stiletto heels."

"What color eyes?"

"Brown, I think. The lighting wasn't too good. She wore a lot of mascara."

"Height?"

"Medium. We were eye to eye."

"Anything else about her stick out in your mind?"

"No." Shannon thought hard, mentally replaying the incident until that moment when the woman had removed her black leather glove and opened her purse, pulling out the ID. Something niggled in her memory. "That's all I can remember."

"Hopefully it'll be enough. Have you still got Mary Calder's original ID?"

"Yes, it's in the cottage."

"Good." He scooped up some papers sitting on the workbench. Shannon had no idea what they were. "We might be able to pick up a fingerprint that will tell us this woman's identity. If she's a prostitute, she probably has a record. It might give us a lead on who's taken Samantha. Mary was assaulted about an hour before you bought her ID. It couldn't have changed many hands in that hour."

Panic spiraled through her at the implication of this bit of news as she ran out into the yard after him. "You're bringing in the police, aren't you, no matter what the note said or how I feel about it? She's my daughter!''

Luke didn't break stride. ''Actually I'm still hoping you'll make the call. It's the best thing you can do for Samantha and the best thing you can do for you. And I think you know that.''

He reached the front steps of the cottage and paused. Shannon saw genuine pain in his eyes. ''It's your choice. Shannon Mulligan didn't have a perfect life, but it was honest and it was hers. And Mary Calder's family would like to put her memory to rest.''

Shannon felt the tears burn her eyes and her throat. No matter how deceived she felt or how angry she was with him, she knew that he sincerely shared her concern for her daughter's welfare. She had to take a chance. He was a cop. And her heart still trusted that he would do everything in his power to bring her baby home safely. ''I want to be Shannon again and I want my baby back. I'll make the call first, then get Mary's ID.''

Shannon bounded up the steps ahead on him, Luke right on her heels.

She didn't see the electrical cord that had been stretched across the doorway until she'd already tripped over it. She was on the floor before she saw the man poised near the door, a hammer raised to strike. She cried out to warn Luke, but it was too late. The hammer connected with his head and he fell to the floor, landing on top of her.

Chapter Eleven

"Luke!" Shannon reached backward ineffectually, trying to rouse him. His weight was crushing her, pinning her to the floor. Was he dead? Where was the cell phone he'd had with him in the workshop?

The cold muzzle of a gun prodded her painfully in the temple. "Don't move and don't scream or you'll never see your baby again."

Shannon's heart quivered like a trapped animal. She tried to look upward to see their assailant, but all she could see from this angle was the floor and a layer of dust coating the blue baseboard molding on the wall she was facing. "Samantha? You have Samantha?"

"Yes. I'm sure you would like to see her?" There was a calculated edge to his words that brought terror to her heart.

Shannon tried not to let the panic seep into her voice. Hadn't Luke told her not to believe anything a criminal said? "Is she all right?"

"She's fine. She misses her mother. But you must come with me if you want her to live to her next birthday." She heard the man grunt as he rolled Luke's body off her. "Don't move yet."

Shannon did as she was told. What was he doing—patting Luke down to see if he was carrying any weapons? He made an "ah" sound as if he'd found something. "I'm going to give you some tape," the man continued a few agonizing seconds later. "You tape his hands and his legs together." A roll of gray duct tape dropped onto the floor beside her. "Hurry."

Luke was on his back, blood seeping from a wound in the right side of his head, behind his ear. Shannon taped his hands together in front of him. At least she could feel a faint pulse in his wrist! *Please live,* she pleaded silently, squeezing his arm. No matter that he was a cop and he'd lied to her. Being arrested seemed the least of her problems now. She knew he cared about her and Samantha. If only she'd listened to him earlier and called the police when he'd forced the issue, there would be help on the way now! Discreetly she looked for Luke's cell phone, but couldn't find it. She wrapped the tape several times around Luke's ankles and tore it.

"Done," she said, risking a glance up at the man. She'd never seen him before. But his salt-and-pepper hair told her that he must be the man Luke had spotted tailing them. He was dressed in expensive fitness wear—black pants and a black muscle shirt, a gold chain circling his beefy neck and a black leather pouch fastened around his waist. He was not what she would call a handsome man, but his features were striking, the bullish eyes, flat cheekbones and broad nose commanding a second look. His eyes, however, black as tar pits, frightened her.

"Toss me the tape."

She did, thinking as she did so that the request was a bad omen. He zipped the tape into the pouch around his waist. ''Can I take the diaper bag?'' she asked, testing the lack of humanity she saw in those eyes. ''Samantha will probably need a bottle and a diaper change. The bag is there on the stool. You'll find a bottle of juice already prepared in the refrigerator.''

He motioned with the gun. ''Get it quickly. We're leaving and walking to my car. If you do or say anything to attract attention, I assure you you'll regret it.''

The thought of being reunited with her daughter gave her legs the strength to step over Luke's prone body and grab the diaper bag, then walk the few steps to the refrigerator to retrieve the bottle.

''Give me the bag.'' He searched it, thrusting one big hand into it. Satisfied it contained nothing more than the bottle, diapers, wipes and a change of clothes, he threw it back at her. ''Out the door. Slowly.''

Shannon slipped the strap of the diaper bag over her left shoulder and moved toward the door. ''Where are we going?'' she dared to ask, hoping Luke might have regained consciousness and be able to send help.

''No questions. Move.''

So much for plan A. She'd have to figure out a plan B.

She pushed the screen door open, careful not to look behind her. There on the railing were her bottles of acrylic paint. Rotating her shoulders to block his view of her left hand, she closed her fingers around the bottle of orange paint she'd used for the scarecrows' noses, then slipped her hand beneath the diaper bag as if holding the bag against her hip. With a flick of her thumbnail, she opened the cap and prayed there was enough paint in the bottle to leave a trail to wherever the man's car was parked.

To her relief, the man moved abreast of her once they'd descended the stairs, using the diaper bag to shield the gun he held near her left hip.

Shannon squeezed the plastic bottle and hoped a dab of paint dropped onto the ground. For good measure, she tried another squeeze. As long as the paint didn't land on her captor's shoes and he didn't look back and spot the orange drops, she might just get away with it.

They stayed off the path, weaving a course through the trees behind her cottage. Shannon could hear the splashing and cries of bathers in the water as they passed within hearing distance of the beach. He must have parked his car near the public road that passed near the private beach. Picnickers often parked alongside the road and walked down to the lake. Shannon kept her sanity by counting and squeezing the bottle every five strides.

Instead of walking in the open along the road toward the few cars that were parked, the man urged her to keep behind the vegetation that bordered the road, making it difficult for any passing cars to see them clearly. Fear that he'd kill her here, now that he'd lured her away from her cottage with promises of reuniting her with her daughter, reared in Shannon's soul. But a few minutes later they came upon the green sedan parked in the shade of a trembling aspen.

Her heart stopped and dread curdled in her veins

when he opened the trunk of the vehicle and told her to climb in. Was this it? Would he kill her now?

"Do you want to see your daughter?"

"Yes, please," Shannon whispered, quaking as those black eyes impaled her.

"Then get in."

"Can't I just ride—"

His left hand flew up and caught her throat, pinching until she was gagging for breath and her vision blurred. "Are you going to get in the trunk?"

She nodded weakly, even as her mind raced with cautions to keep the bottle of paint hidden from view as she climbed into the trunk, the diaper bag clasped to her.

The trunk closed on her, shutting out light and shutting out hope. How long could she breathe in here without suffocating?

The will to live had her running her fingers over the inside of the trunk, searching for something she could use as a weapon to surprise her captor. Was there enough paint in the bottle to squirt in his face when he opened the trunk? She found the indentation of a taillight and the wires that lit the brake lights. Shannon ripped at the wires until she felt them pull through the opening. She could feel the car bouncing over the uneven ground as it made its way back to the road. Maybe a police car would notice his brake lights weren't operating properly and pull him over to give him a ticket. She pulled out the wires for the other brake light. Even better, maybe she could break the plastic with something and draw attention to the fact that someone was in the trunk of the car. She could wiggle her fingers or squeeze paint through the opening...

Inspired by the idea that she might be able to continue leaving a paint trail, Shannon went on with her fumbling search of the vehicle. There must be something she could use... She found some kind of nylon zippered bag. Inside, her fingers identified jumper cables.

The clamps would be hard enough to do the job. Shannon shoved one of them through the hole as hard as she could, jamming it at the plastic covering until she heard something crack. A shaft of daylight the size of a golfball told her she'd succeeded. There were no cars on the road behind them, though. Groping for the bottle of paint, she slid it through the opening and squeezed, praying the laws of physics would be with her and the drops would land on the roadway, not on the bumper of the car.

Please, God, this had to work!

WHAT THE HELL had hit him? Luke felt as if a marching band was holding tryouts in his skull. Vaguely he remembered coming through the door with Shannon, then a movement on his right before someone cracked his head open. *Shannon.* Where was she?

Luke listened to the sounds in the cottage to make sure that the assailant wasn't lurking nearby before he opened his eyes. God, he'd blown this. He'd let himself get personally involved with Shannon, let that tailor his judgment. If she was dead... Luke cautiously opened his eyes. He couldn't see Shannon on the floor in his field of vision. Fear that she might be lying elsewhere—maybe brutally assaulted as his wife had been—had his head turning toward the inside of Shannon's cottage. Nausea swirled through him, burning acidly as it rose in his throat. His vision fogged, then cleared. Luke saw table legs and stool legs, maybe more than were actually there, but no human legs.

"Shannon! Are you there?"

Luke couldn't hear a reply over the pounding in his head. He had to move. Get assistance. The fog settling in his brain slowed him from realizing that his legs and arms were bound. Damn, he'd roll, instead.

Choking on bile, he rolled across the floor toward the kitchen counter, stopping when his body slammed into the cabinets. Waves of dizziness kept rolling through his head. The phone was mounted on the wall at the end of the counter, but he should be able to snag it down by the cord. His first attempt to lift his arms toward the cord failed, but on his second try his fingers tangled in the coils and the phone slipped from its base and clattered to the floor. He used a pinkie to punch in 911.

He managed to identify himself and state the emergency—and ask for Staff Sergeant Rayford's assistance—before he blacked out again.

THE CAR DREW to a halt. Adrenaline spiked through Shannon as the engine was extinguished. Would he remove her from the trunk? She pulled the bottle of paint out of the taillight and tucked it into the side pocket of the diaper bag. The car door opened and slammed, the sedan rocking from the motion. Shannon tensed, counting off the seconds as she waited for him to open the trunk. Would he notice the broken tail-light?

A curse, followed by the violent impact of his fists on the trunk told her the exact moment he spotted the broken taillight. Shannon screamed, unable to stop the rush of terror at the rumble of steel over her head.

"You bitch! I told you..."

The trunk opened, and Shannon wanted to cringe at the rage twisting his features. But she didn't.

"I needed to breathe. There wasn't enough air," she said defiantly.

He gripped her arm roughly, pulling her from the trunk. "Come on, get out."

Shannon's legs, cramped from the position she'd been in, gave way as she climbed out. She stumbled on the rocky drive, feeling pins and needles as her circulation started to return. His viselike hold on her arm kept her from hitting the ground as he yanked her toward a clapboard home, its yellow paint showing signs of wear. Shannon didn't dare look back at the sedan's bumper to see if signs of the paint she'd used were evident. A wide balcony—stained nut brown—jutted from the second floor of the house to take advantage of the spectacular view. They'd driven into the hills above Kettle Lake, and the terrain was more barren. The harsh landscape of grass and rock was alleviated only by the dark green fringe of ponderosa pine and the blue-violet flowers on the clumps of sage-brush.

She dropped the bottle of paint into a straggly bush near the downstairs entrance. Fear cramped her stomach as they entered the house through a door that didn't appear locked, stepping into a brown-tiled foyer. The house smelled of bacon grease and stale beer. Ahead of her, a dingy carpeted staircase led up to the second floor. Was Samantha being held here? Shannon listened for her daughter's familiar sounds, praying her baby was unharmed.

"Where's my daughter? You promised you'd bring me to her."

Her captor slapped her on the back of the head. Shannon bit her lip to keep from crying out. She was done cowering to men who thought they had control over her because they were bigger and stronger. "She's here. She's fine." Instead of taking her upstairs, he pushed her down a hallway wallpapered with a brown-and-gold geometric pattern that was as dated as the gold shag carpet. There were three doors painted a shade of marigold, all of them closed. Her captor stopped at the first door on the right and opened it. A blind was drawn at the window, dimming the room's interior. But she could see a new-looking portable crib jammed between two single beds.

Inside the crib her daughter slept on her stomach, her head turned away. Shannon tried to go to her, needing to reassure herself that her daughter was breathing. "Saman—"

Her captor clamped a hand over her mouth and pushed her against the wall in the corridor. "Shut up. I don't want you to wake her. Do you understand?"

Shannon nodded, gagging on the taste of his sweaty flesh.

He removed his hand.

She stared up into those black soulless eyes. "What do you want from me?"

A cruel smile pulled at his lips and he gestured toward the second door. "Down here."

Visions of being physically or sexually assaulted rampaged in her mind. But she'd survived both before. And she would again. Survival was all that mattered—until she could find a way to rescue Samantha and escape. And she could cling to the slim hope that Luke would somehow find them.

But nothing she'd endured in her life had prepared her for the hysteria that seized her when her captor opened the door to the other room and she saw the person stretched out on the bed, lying in wait for her.

It was Rob.

Chapter Twelve

Luke could have sworn Shannon was calling his name. But when he roused himself from unconsciousness, the woman cutting the duct tape from his wrists was Constable Reed, the female RCMP officer who'd acted as a courier drop.

"Try to stay awake," the constable advised him, cutting the tape that bound his legs. "You could have a concussion. Support units are on the way. So is an ambulance."

"Mary?" Luke struggled to sit up, to find her himself. The pounding in his head prevented him from moving too quickly. "Where is—"

Constable Reed's eyes were serious beneath the brim of her forage cap. "There's no sign of her on the premises. Or the child. You told the dispatcher there'd been an abduction and an assault. You're the only one here."

"He got her, too, then."

"Who's he? Can you describe your attacker?" The constable rose, pulling open drawers in the kitchen until she found one that held dish towels. She bent down beside him, pressing the towel to his head.

Luke took it from her. "There's ice in the freezer. I didn't see whoever hit me. It might be Mary's ex-husband, Rob Barrie. There's a history of domestic violence. He did time for stalking and there's a No Communication Order in effect. Mary found a note in the crib when she discovered the baby was missing. But there's a possible other suspect." Luke took the ice pack she offered from the freezer, then filled her in on the details of his wife's murder and what Shannon had told him about purchasing his wife's identity, while the constable furiously scribbled notes in her notebook.

"Do you have any pictures of the victims?"

"No, none."

A man's voice called from outside, "Mary? I saw the police car. Is everything all right in there?"

Luke exchanged a glance with the constable. "It's Bill Oakes—he's the caretaker of Shady Pines."

The constable rose and moved to the door, her tone authoritative and brooking no argument. "Sir, please do not enter the scene. But I'd like to ask you a few questions." She exited the screen door. Luke heard Bill's distressed exclamations when the constable informed him that Mary and Samantha had been abducted and Luke assaulted. "Is Luke all right?"

"Just a bump, Bill," Luke called out, trying to stand. The ice helped dull the pounding. His legs didn't feel as if they had any connection to the rest of his body, but he got himself to his feet. Bill might have seen something that could indicate where Shannon and Samantha had been taken. Luke staggered to the screen door. "Have you seen Mary or Samantha—or anything suspicious?"

Bill scratched his head, his eyes sorrowful as he took in Luke's bloodied appearance. "Can't say as I've seen Mary or the baby, but you might want to have a look over here." Bill pointed at something on the ground near his feet. "Looks like orange paint, and it goes off toward those trees. That's what brought me over here. I was out walking, spotted it and wondered what it was. I followed it here to Mary's cottage."

In the distance came the wail of a siren. Luke brushed against one of the scarecrows Mary had been painting on the front porch and nearly fell down the stairs in his haste to see what Bill was talking about. Finally he saw it, a dab of orange no bigger than a dime on the grass. Then another a few feet away. Luke grabbed Bill's shoulder. "Show us where they lead."

Constable Reed put a staying hand on his forearm. "I'll check it out. You need medical attention."

"Not a chance," Luke replied bluntly. "This is a joint forces investigation, and I'm going every step of the way." Ice pack clutched to his head, eyes focused on to the ground, he followed Bill's shuffling gate, hope burgeoning in his heart.

The facts and the law be damned. You had to love a woman smart enough to leave a trail.

SHANNON FOUGHT with everything in her when her captor tried to force her toward the bed. Rob was lying deathly still on his side, his arms bound behind him. A thin cord was wrapped around his legs and tied to the black metal footboard of the bed. Her captor grabbed one of her arms, wrenching it painfully up behind her until she felt certain it would snap. He pushed her facefirst onto the bed, his knee digging into her back.

Shannon heard the sound of duct tape being pulled. *He must have put down the gun.* She squirmed, trying to buck him off her. But the weight of his body pushed relentlessly into her.

"Mary, Mary, quite contrary," he grunted, "escaped her fate and lived to regret it." The tape snared her wrist. Shannon cried out in despair as he grabbed her other arm and jerked it back behind her. He'd called her Mary. Did that imply he thought she was Mary Calder and this was Mary Calder's killer?

"Why are you doing this?"

"Why?" He laughed. "I would think that was obvious. I couldn't take the chance you could identify me. You would have gotten away with faking your death if your husband hadn't followed you to British Columbia. I've been keeping an eye on him. Pays to have friends in high places."

Her husband? Shannon tried to make sense of what he was saying. Maybe he *didn't* think she was the real Mary Calder. Had Rob told this man she'd faked her death when she'd disappeared? Maybe Rob had hired this lunatic because he didn't want to risk—

"Seems to me I'm doing your husband a favor. Does the good constable know you've been sleeping with someone behind his back? My guess is that the baby isn't even his."

Now Shannon was totally confused. The good constable? Rob wasn't a police officer. The only police officer she knew was Luke. Her captor's knee rotated forty-five degrees. One of his hands clamped around her ankle. Oh, God, was he going to tape her legs, too? Shannon kicked furiously in hopes of avoiding this final restriction.

His fist slammed into the side of her head, stunning her. ''Quit kicking me, bitch. You're not escaping death a second time. Only this time we'll do it right—real romanticlike with your jilted lover in bed beside you. I'll let him take the credit.''

Shannon felt as if a key had turned in a lock, opening a door to a vault of knowledge. If this man thought Rob was her jilted lover, then the cop he was referring to could only be Luke. Which meant that Luke was Mary Calder's husband!

Why hadn't he told her?

Why should he? He was a cop trying to find out who'd murdered his wife. Ready to do anything, even seduce his wife's imposter, to bring an end to the unanswered questions. How he must have felt to look at her, knowing what a liar she was. Sympathy for his loss twined with the terror filling her soul.

No wonder Luke had seen through all her attempts at misdirection. She should be angry at him, but that only made her a hypocrite. She'd brought all this on herself. Maybe Luke would die, too, because of her mistakes.

Her captor pushed her onto her left side so that she was facing Rob. Though he'd bound her legs together with the duct tape, she kicked at him as he passed a length of cord over the tape and tried to knot it to the footboard. "Listen to me, you're making a mistake! I've never seen you before in my life. I'm not Mary Calder. My name is Shannon Mulligan. And this man beside me is my ex-husband, Robert Barrie. That's our daughter, Samantha, in the other room. Mary Calder is the identity I took on to keep my ex from finding me, because we were having problems. Please, just leave us alone. I promise I won't say anything about what's happened here."

"It has always amazed me how you PR people can spin fairy tales at the drop of a hat." He flicked his gaze at Rob. "I saw him sniffing around you at night. Him and the other one. Wasn't long before you invited your husband back into your bed, too. You're screwing three different men and you think I'm going to believe a word you say?"

Shannon chose to ignore his outrageous claim. The man obviously had his facts wrong. "Did Rob take Samantha? Or did you?"

He slapped a piece of tape over her mouth. "You figure it out."

Shannon watched helplessly as he left the room, leaving the door ajar. What was he planning to do now?

She inched forward on the bed, butting Rob with her shoulder, hoping to rouse him. All these years she'd been running from him, and now she wanted his help in saving their lives. His features were slack, indicating he was unconscious and not merely asleep. The thick stubble coating his jaw suggested he hadn't shaved in days. Had he been captive that long? She lifted herself onto her hip, examining him. She saw a dark bruise and swelling where his right temple rested on the rust-and-gold bedspread. She also saw dirt stains on his black jeans and black T-shirt, but no other clues that might indicate how long he'd been in Blossom Valley.

After everything he'd done to her, she should have wanted to kill him, but all she felt was sorrow that the promises and expectations they'd had of each other had come down to this. She heard footsteps in the hallway and quickly lay back down. Her captor entered, carrying an armload of pine needles and brush. He deposited it on the floor near Rob's side of the bed. Then he went out again. What was he doing?

Shannon heard her daughter whimper, then cry out. The sound of her distress tore at Shannon's heart. The man reappeared in the bedroom for an instant to retrieve the diaper bag, then disappeared. Shannon strained her ears trying to figure out what was happening in the other room with her daughter. She heard the low murmur of conversation. Was someone else in the house, or was he talking to Samantha as he gave her a bottle or changed her diaper? It was difficult to tell over Samantha's cries.

Instantly Samantha's fussing stopped. He must have given her a bottle.

The sunlight had faded to dusky shadows before the man returned, carrying another armload of wood and brush, which he proceeded to spread around the bed. Shannon could no longer see Rob's watch, so she didn't know how much time had passed since she'd been abducted. It would be dark soon, which meant no one could follow the trail she'd tried to leave—

provided Luke had regained consciousness and alerted the authorities. To keep herself from going completely insane while her captor made six more trips to collect brush and sticks, Shannon tuned her senses to her daughter's precious babbling in the other room and prayed that Luke would find them before her captor put a match to the kindling.

TIME. LUKE COULD FEEL each excruciating second slipping away as if each were a shard of glass being extracted from his brow. They'd followed the drops of orange paint through the woods. And a chasm of fear had opened wide within him when the drops ended abruptly near a set of tire tracks. A car had obviously pulled off the road. They'd hurried to the road, hoping to find more tire tracks that might indicate which direction the vehicle had turned. But reached a dead end.

The shoulder here was dry and compact. No marks.

The police spread out to knock on the doors of the few residences along the road to see if anyone had seen a vehicle. Luke weighed the chances of finding Shannon and Samantha as he rested in the front seat of a patrol car in between consults with the RCMP corporal who'd been sent in to supervise the situation. An EMT had checked Luke out, but Luke refused to be transported to hospital to have his head injury examined by a doctor.

Corporal Donaldson, who was built like a Land Rover and had a face as smooth as soapstone, studied a map of the area that he'd spread out on the hood of the car. Luke had already pegged him as an officer who knew his job and did it with logic and efficiency.

Everything possible was being done. Roadblocks had been established to keep Shannon and Samantha's abductor from transporting them out of the area, and a helicopter was in the air, keeping an eye out for a green sedan driving too quickly. The dog squad had picked up Shannon's scent, leading her handler to the exact spot where the paint trail had ended near the tire tracks. The Ident Section had been called in to comb the cottage for forensic evidence.

But still the fear cut Luke deep, chafing his heart raw, that the next time he saw Shannon would be in the morgue. His heart lurched when the patrol car's radio suddenly crackled to life. Luke copied every word of the radio transmission. An officer had spotted a thin line of orange paint on the pavement farther down the road.

They still had a lead!

Donaldson responded to the call, issuing orders to the officers under his command. Then he folded the map and jumped into the vehicle, lights flashing as he started the engine and made a rapid U-turn. As if by a miracle, the officer who'd just called in came back on the radio, "There's more right up to the highway."

"Amazing," Donaldson muttered. He responded to the call on the car radio. "Keep your eyes open, Taylor. It might be a trap, or someone could be trying to lead us in the opposite direction. Copy."

Luke, however, had no doubts. He'd experienced Shannon's survival instincts firsthand. "It's her."

Once they reached the highway, the paint was harder to spot, the dribbles appearing farther apart. Traffic was blocked off as they pursued the trail at

what felt like a snail's pace. The sun was sinking behind the hills, and still there was no sign the vehicle
had turned off the highway. They were in a race
against nightfall and the ever-present possibility that
the trail might suddenly end—leaving them with nothing to follow.

SHANNON KNEW THE END was near when her captor
entered the bedroom lugging the portable crib. Samantha was seated in it, her eyes wide with confusion.
He'd promised Shannon he wouldn't harm her baby.
She thrashed on the bed. "Nnn… Nnn…"

Her protests were ineffectual against the tape covering her mouth. Samantha must have picked up on
Shannon's terror, for her face screwed up and she let
out a wail. She rose unsteadily, her fingers gripping
the mesh sides of the crib. Shannon's eyes brimmed
with helpless tears at the fear on her daughter's face
and in her cry. She'd failed to keep her baby safe!

Her captor's mouth pulled into a cruel smile as he
patted her thigh. "Not to worry, Mary. The smoke
should knock you out before the flames reach you."

Shannon lifted her legs and tried to kick him to get
the disgusting feel of his latex-gloved fingers off her,
but the cord anchoring her feet to the footboard prevented her from making contact.

Laughing, her captor opened a door to a closet and
pulled out a case of beer. To her horror, he twisted
open the cap and splashed the contents over the pile
of brush he'd arranged on the floor. Then he pressed
Rob's fingers around the empty bottle and dropped it
on the floor. Steadily he worked through the case, oc-

casionally throwing a bottle at the far wall so that it shattered and fell to the floor, sending Samantha into hysterics.

Ignoring Samantha's cries, her captor took a knife and removed Rob's bonds, stuffing the rope and tape into a plastic bag. Then he arranged a partially emptied beer bottle in Rob's fingers. With a satisfied smirk, he withdrew a box of matches from his pocket.

Shannon smelled the sulfur as the match ignited.

"Sorry I won't be attending the funeral, Mary. I have another engagement." The match fell from his fingers and the brush leaped to fiery life on the side of the room nearest the doorway. He watched it for a moment, then left them to die.

As soon as she heard him run down the hall, Shannon twisted into action, rolling over and grappling for the beer bottle in Rob's hand. When her fingers found purchase, she curled up, hoping she wouldn't fall off the bed as she forced her wrists to pass over her backside until she could sit up, her wrists beneath her bent knees. The fire greedily ignited, flaring waist-high and sending out a wave of heat that seemed to intensify with each passing second. Like a living thing the fire moved, licking at the floor, leaping up as it hit dry tinder or suddenly smoldering as it encountered beer-soaked brush. Shannon had assumed the beer would feed the flames, but it cast off smoke, instead. Dangerous smoke that rose like writhing serpents and gathered at the ceiling. So little time left before the whole room was engulfed in flames.

Samantha's cries echoing in her ears, Shannon spread her knees wide, shot her arms through the opening and smashed the bottle on the footboard. Beer splashed over her legs. Another smash gave her a jagged but serviceable knife that quickly pierced the tape ensnaring her ankles. She ripped the tape off her mouth, coughing as she inhaled acrid smoke. "It's okay, baby. Mommy's here." There was no time to cut the tape that bound her wrists. The wall of flames had spread around the bed and separated her from Samantha. She leaped off the bed, panic spurting through her as she tugged the bedspread out from beneath Rob's body and dropped it over a section of flames, smothering them long enough to dart over her makeshift bridge.

It was another feat of gymnastics to stoop over the portable crib, her elbows parted as she shimmied her arms down Samantha's body and lifted her. Nothing had ever felt more precious than her daughter gathered to her breast.

The heat was unbearable. Shannon staggered, coughing and choking, trying to draw breath. Despair assaulted her when she saw the flames licking across the bedding toward Rob's body. More flames blocked the way to the door, creeping closer. The window was their only hope....

Chapter Thirteen

It was a scene from a Halloween nightmare—the unholy glow of flames at the window of the darkened house. Guns drawn, the police converged on the residence. Luke felt as if he'd been pulled out of his body, and his heart was in a state of arrest as he and Donaldson awaited word or the sound of gunshots to tell them what was happening in the house.

Suddenly he heard the sound of glass shattering, and Donaldson had to hold him back as two constables pulled Shannon out of the window, Samantha clutched in her arms.

But Luke broke free of Donaldson's grasp, not feeling his legs as he rushed behind an EMT to the spot where Shannon was being laid on the ground a safe distance from the house, Samantha still in her arms.

"Shannon, I'm here." Luke dropped to his knees beside her head, stroking her hair as a constable extricated Samantha, kicking and coughing, from Shannon's arms. Shannon's eyes were closed, and he couldn't tell if she was breathing on her own. Luke reached for the baby. "I'll hold her. She knows me.

How's the mother?'' he asked the EMT, who was checking Shannon's vital signs.

"Breathing. And we got a pulse."

"Thank God." Luke cradled Samantha close to his heart, trying to calm her with his voice and his hands. Not aware that he was crying. They were alive. That was all that mattered.

SHANNON BARELY REMEMBERED answering questions in the emergency room. She was so tired. The doctor who had checked her out had told her she needed to wear an oxygen mask for four to six hours to remove the carbon monoxide from her system. The big cop who'd interrogated her reminded her of one of those muscled Hollywood-action film stars with a brain like a steel trap. He told her that Luke was also in the emergency room receiving treatment for his head injury and that her baby was fine. But her ex-husband had not survived the fire. The rest seemed incoherent—trying to convince the big cop that Rob, too, had been abducted by Mary Calder's killer. Trying to provide a description of the man who'd tried to kill them and recalling what her abductor had said to her in those horrible hours—whether he'd mentioned a motive for killing Mary Calder.

She was relieved when the doctor chased the big cop away.

Glad to drift off, safe at last in the knowledge that she had found peace from Rob.

SHANNON SENSED Luke's presence beside her bed before she opened her eyes. Like a pond in a tranquil setting, he exuded an aura of calm that beckoned her soul to wake from its rest. Face him, knowing what she'd done. Knowing who he was. It was the next step to reclaiming the woman she used to be.

Someone had removed the oxygen mask she'd fallen asleep wearing last night. The fear that he would condemn her evaporated as her lashes fluttered open and she met those serious gray-blue irises square on. She also saw the bandage on his head that only made him seem more ruggedly appealing. Gratitude that her captor hadn't seriously harmed him stole through her like a trickle of warm water.

"Shannon?"

"Saman—" Her voice was mildly hoarse.

Luke squeezed her fingers briefly. "She's fine. Smoke inhalation, but nothing to worry about. A mild burn, like you. The nurses are doting on her and your mother and aunt are flying in. Rob's probation officer gave us their names. The doctor called them, and they'll be here this afternoon."

"That other cop told me Rob is dead."

"Yes. A combination of head injury, smoke and flames. Thought you might like to know that we found some photocopies of pictures in his wallet. Pictures of Samantha at Christmas and your truck."

Shannon closed her eyes. She knew the pictures he was talking about. The ones she'd sent care of her mother's bridge friend so her mother and aunt could see Samantha. She told Luke about the pictures and the extraordinary precautions she'd taken. "I don't know how Rob found me through those. Even if he'd been following my mother and broke into her friend's house and stole them, there was no identifying information on the photos that could lead him to me. I made sure the license plate of my pickup wasn't visible, or the name of my company. The woman didn't even know my address. Though I suppose if she'd forgotten to destroy the envelope the photos came in, there might have been a postmark. And I think my mother's friend or my mother might have noticed if the photos went missing. My mother plays bridge every Thursday afternoon.''

''Actually, I don't think your mother's friend is to blame. One of the photos of your truck was enlarged. And in the enlargement, if you look carefully, you can see 'The Garden Patch Collection' reflected in the side passenger mirror. It probably took him a while, but my guess is that's how he tracked you down. And he probably only kept the originals long enough to have them photocopied, then replaced them.''

''I feel so stupid.''

''That is a word I would never use to describe you. The local police will be talking about that paint trail you left for the next twenty years.''

Shannon flushed at the accolade. The mild burn— similar to a sunburn—she'd received from the flames made her ultrasensitive to the heat flooding her face.

Whatever warmth she'd sensed in Luke's tone was quickly reined in. ''I'd like to ask you some questions about what happened.''

She nodded stiffly. ''Who's asking questions? Luke Mathews, undercover cop? Or Mary Calder's husband? I figured out who you are. He—the man who took me—kept referring to my husband. I finally realized he meant you, not Rob.'' Her fingers twisted in the sheets.

Luke studied her intently before replying. Shannon felt her anxiety skyrocket. ''My name is Luke Calder. And I am a cop, but my investigation into my wife's murder has been strictly unofficial. Corporal Donaldson is in charge of investigating your abduction and Rob's murder and working with the Ottawa authorities. I'm just a witness cooperating fully with the investigation. I'm asking you these questions as a man who'd like to know what happened to his wife. But you would be wise to consult with a lawyer before you talk to me further. Anything you've told me since we met or that you might tell me now...I might be called upon to testify about under oath. And you should know that if you hadn't decided to go to the police when Samantha was kidnapped, then I would have had to. You'd told me that you'd committed a crime, and I would have had to report that because I'm an officer of the law.''

Shannon gaped at him. ''Is that why you kept insisting that I go to the police with the whole story when Samantha was kidnapped?''

''One of several reasons. But mostly because I felt that your best chance of getting Samantha back safely was with police help. And I knew it would be better for you in the long run if you turned yourself in.''

''I confessed everything to Corporal Donaldson last night. And I don't need to talk to a lawyer to tell you what you have a right to know, Luke. I was so scared! You were right. The man who abducted me thought I was your wife, and he admitted to trying to kill her.

I'm so sorry about what happened to your Mary. And so sorry that I took her name." Shannon wanted to reach out and touch him, but shame kept her fingers knotted in the sheets. "It must have been so painful for you to be around me, knowing what I liar I was."

"I don't condone what you did, Shannon. But I understand that you did what you felt you had to do. I know you had nothing to do with my wife's murder. Did he give you any indication why he killed her?"

Shannon shook her head. "No. He just seemed angry that she thought she could outsmart him. He thought I was having an affair with Rob, and he staged the fire to make it look as if Rob was jealous I was going back to you. It was very confusing. Have the police caught him yet?"

"No, but I was told that Rob had been renting the house where you were taken—he'd been there about three weeks. The owner identified him from a picture. He used a company name to rent the house and a car. I suspect he was waiting until his probation and the No Communication Order to expire before approaching you…which would have been today."

Shannon told herself not to dwell on whatever Rob might have had planned for a family reunion. "I'd forgotten the exact date it expired. The man who abducted me said something very confusing about two men sniffing around my cottage at night. He must have meant Rob and Dylan."

"It could explain why Dylan seemed so shocked when I accused him of the break-in at Glorie's. Maybe Rob did it. We might learn more when your abductor is apprehended."

"So he's still out there somewhere?"

"'Fraid so. And they don't have any solid leads. Donaldson will most likely be back to interview you again sometime this morning. But, Shannon, you should really consult with a lawyer before you answer any of his questions."

Shannon felt a spasm of alarm at the warning edge in his voice when he'd mentioned a lawyer. Her gaze slid over the firm line of his jaw up to the bandage on his head. "Am I going to be arrested?"

Her question hung in the air between them, stiff as one of the starched bed linens. She saw the muscles knot in his throat. Amazing to think that she'd kissed him, that she'd wanted him to make love to her. That even now she felt the physical ache of loss at knowing that the Luke Mathews she'd grown close to—and had fantasized about—hadn't been real. That he'd probably testify against her in a court of law.

His eyes flashed with an emotion that might have been regret. Or was it perhaps resignation that the end of a bitter experience had at last been reached? "Chances are you'll be arrested once the doctor says you're ready to be released. Should that happen before your mother and aunt arrive, they'll put Samantha in the care of child services. But you can avert that possibility by making arrangements before it comes to that. I'll take her if you can't make other suitable arrangements."

Shannon stared at him, deeply moved by his offer. Mary Calder had had sterling taste in men. "You would do that after everything I've done?"

"The Crown prosecutor probably won't like it, but

Samantha knows me. Better with me than with complete strangers. And it should only be for a few hours. I'm hoping the doctor won't release either of you until your mother and aunt arrive.'' He leaned forward. ''I won't lie to you, Shannon. Because of your flight history, they'll detain you until your first appearance before a judge. That could be later today or tomorrow morning. Then it's up to the judge to determine whether you'll be held for trial. You need to speak to a lawyer to discuss your options. Bill and Alice dropped off a change of clothes for you. They're in a bag in the bathroom. I thought you'd want to shower and wear clothes that didn't smell of smoke.''

She noticed now that he'd changed clothes, too. There had been blood on his T-shirt and jeans yesterday.

''Okay, I'll hire a lawyer. Thank you.'' She'd survived near-certain death. She could survive being arrested. It was no less than she deserved.

''In the meantime,'' Luke continued, his tone shifting back into neutral, ''an RCMP constable has been posted at the door of your hospital room for your protection.''

Her pulse spiked. ''Do you think he'll come back?''

''It's a possibility we have to consider. You're the only witness to what he's done. And he admitted to you that he'd killed my wife.''

She shuddered at the thought of that man roaming free. ''I want him caught as soon as possible. For your sake. And mine. I've traded one nightmare for another.''

Luke had never been so conflicted in his feelings as

he was now, gazing down at Shannon dwarfed in the hospital bed, her face pink from her burn, struggling to be strong in the face of certain arrest. "Well, I haven't given up on finding your abductor. I brought some pictures I'd like you to look at."

Luke didn't know how to react to the compassion in Shannon's eyes as he told her about his wife's career as a public-relations consultant and explained his theory that her abductor and Mary's killer might be someone he'd met at one of the many business, social or charity events he'd attended with his wife. "The guy who'd tailed us in town looked familiar to me, but I haven't been able to place his face yet." He lifted a thick courier's envelope from her bedside table, which Donaldson had delivered when he'd dropped by Luke's hospital room to update him on the search for the suspect. "My wife's secretary culled together these photos from the events my wife attended in the last few months of her life, plus some other pictures she gathered elsewhere. I'd like you to have a look at them with me. See if you recognize anyone."

Shannon held out her hands. "Let me at 'em."

Luke didn't tell her that he and Corporal Donaldson had already gone through them looking for anyone who matched the description she'd given of her attacker. They'd found at least a dozen potential matches—some definite maybes, but none that Luke could say with absolute certainty was the suspect who'd tailed them. His glimpse of the suspect had been only that—a glimpse.

Maybe Shannon would have better luck.

They started sifting through the stack of photos.

Some were actual newspaper clippings, others were photos downloaded from newspaper archives on the Internet. And somehow Erin had collected both black-and-white and color photos taken by professional and amateur photographers. All were labeled. Luke owed her dinner and ballet tickets to thank her for all her effort.

They had worked their way through half the pile in silence when Luke heard Shannon's startled gasp. She tapped the chest of a man second from the left in a group photo. "That's him."

"ARE YOU SURE?"

"He stood a few feet from me, smiling as he dropped the match that started the fire. Yes, I'm sure."

Luke read the name in the caption below the photo: Eldon Winthrop. The name sounded familiar. Luke examined the photo more closely. It had been taken at a business-awards ceremony, which took place two months before his wife's death. Not an event that Luke had attended with Mary. Winthrop was listed as the vice president of the organization.

"Hold on a sec." He used the hospital phone and his calling card to dial his wife's secretary's new office number. His cell phone had disappeared during his attack. "Your package arrived, Erin. Your thoroughness is commendable."

"I was motivated. Did it help?"

"Yes. That's why I'm calling." Luke described the photo Shannon had chosen and read Erin the caption describing the business-awards dinner. "Did Mary attend the event?"

"She certainly did. One of her clients was the recipient of an award that night."

"Does the name Eldon Winthrop ring any bells with you?"

Erin's voice was hesitant. "I don't like the direction this conversation is heading, Luke."

"Just answer the question, please, Erin."

Luke could feel Shannon watching him, listening.

"I've never met him, but he's a client of the firm I'm with now. He's a businessman—commercial real estate. He's involved with several charities around the city. He's not married. One of the secretaries thinks he has a boyfriend."

"Did Mary ever do any work for him?"

"Not to my knowledge, though she would have leaped at the opportunity to run one of the publicity campaigns for some of the charity events he's been involved in. Our firm handled the local-hero golf tournament last summer—pitting cops against firemen, politicians against schoolteachers. The money raised went for university scholarships for deserving students."

Luke felt a tingling sensation between his shoulder blades. Some of the higher-ups in the police department had played in that golf tournament, and he'd seen pictures posted around the station. Had Winthrop been in some of those pictures? But murder? "Thanks, Erin. Don't say a word about this to anyone unless he's carrying a badge and his name is Detective Zach Vaughn."

"What was that all about?" Shannon demanded as he ended the call.

He repeated what Erin had told him.

"But why would someone like that kill your wife?"

"I don't know, but I plan to find out. Erin sent me guest lists along with the photographs."

As Luke slid the lists out of the courier envelope, Shannon pushed the pile of photographs aside. The touch of her fingers on his forearm sent a shaft of awareness pulsing through him. "Give me some of the lists," she said. "It'll be faster if we both look."

They found Winthrop's name on two lists—a New Year's Eve party that Luke and Mary had attended, and an auction in February to benefit a cancer foundation. Only one list remained—the guest list for the St. Patrick's Day party that Mary had stopped in on that fateful night. Coincidentally the party had been held at the same country club that had hosted the golf tournament. Luke gave a strangled cry as he flipped the first sheet over and scanned the names on the next page. Winthrop's name was at the bottom of the list.

It wasn't much of a connection, but Vaughn might think it was enough to do some discreet nosing into Winthrop's current location.

Chapter Fourteen

"Did you say Eldon Winthrop?" Detective Vaughn barked in Luke's ear.

Luke winced at the grating steel of the detective's voice and automatically checked the waiting room to make sure no one was listening in on his call. "Shannon identified him from a photo," he repeated, pushing back. "She seems one hundred percent certain. I believe her."

Vaughn swore. Luke could hear the agitated movement of the detective's office chair over the line. "You have no idea what you're into, Calder."

"Are you implying I'm way off base?"

"No, quite the opposite. God help me, I believe you. I'm just marveling at how two seemingly unrelated events can suddenly seamlessly fit together."

Luke ran his fingers through his hair in frustration. "What the hell are you talking about, Vaughn?"

"The same night your wife was killed, Hugh Jennings, who was a guest at the St. Patrick's Day party, was found dead in a private upstairs lounge at the club. An autopsy was done to determine the cause of death. The coroner thought at first it was an apparent heart attack but the victim's heart looked pretty healthy. When he examined the heart tissues under the microscope, he found subtle signs of potassium-chloride poisoning—signs he normally wouldn't have looked for had the heart shown signs of disease. The potassium chloride would have had to have been injected in order to kill. The coroner found a needle mark in the scalp. When the blood tests came back, they showed evidence of sleeping pills in his blood. So someone slipped him some sleeping pills—probably in a drink at the party—to incapacitate him, then gave him a lethal injection of potassium chloride. Jennings apparently booked the lounge for a private meeting, but we have no witnesses who can tell us who he met in the lounge that night."

"Any suspects?" Luke asked.

"No motive we can dig up on the wife. Friends say they were happily married. She had plenty of family money of her own. She wasn't at the party—she was attending a play at the National Arts Centre that finished at 10 p.m. We have a witness who says she stayed in her seat until just before the end of the performance when she got a call on her cell phone from her husband. The witness was annoyed at the call because you're supposed to turn cell phones and pagers off. The wife claims her husband called to tell her he wasn't feeling well and asked her what time she'd be home that night. The witness clearly heard her say, 'I'll leave now.'

"Still, we've been quietly watching her. We've got a who's-who list of individuals who didn't like the way Jennings did business—apparently you didn't want to cross this guy in negotiations. Half the people on the list simply resented his wealth and the obscene amounts of money he'd throw away on parties and clothing his wife in headline-grabbing costumes on the society pages. But here's where Eldon Winthrop ties in. He was Jennings's business partner. Only thing is, he didn't show up for the party. He called the hostess and told her he couldn't make it. He gave a story about running late after a business meeting and needing to go home to rest because he thought he was coming down with the flu. He can't prove he stayed home that night, but no one saw him at the party, either.''

Luke propped an elbow on top of the pay phone and studied Winthrop's smiling face. ''So he hired someone to do the dirty deed—maybe someone dressed as a waiter.''

''If Winthrop hired someone, he covered his tracks well.''

''Is there any chance he's got something going on the side with Jennings's wife?''

''Doubtful. It's common knowledge his tastes run to men, though he doesn't seem to have had any long-term partners.''

''Could he have had something going with his business partner?''

''We've considered that angle, too,'' Vaughn said. ''But nothing conclusive to back it up. Both men have friends in high places who wouldn't take kindly to unfounded allegations. I'll notify the lead detective in Jennings's murder of this development, and we'll track down Winthrop as soon as possible. It's only a five-hour flight to Ottawa from the west coast. He could have caught a flight last night or this morning. He's going to need a rock-solid alibi to prove where he's been if he's been out of town. Is Corporal Donaldson there with you?"

"Not at the moment, but I'm expecting him soon. He's got reinforcements scouring the area motels, campgrounds and restaurants for anyone fitting the suspect's description."

"I'll call him through official channels and brief him on this latest development. Let him know you have a photograph of the suspect."

Luke ended the call and rubbed his weary eyes. The doctor had told him he had a concussion, and he'd been held overnight for observation. Some nurse had woken him every hour or two, checking his pupils. While his headache had lessened, his head still felt like a dented tin can. Or maybe it was his heart that felt kicked in.

He'd wanted peace. He'd wanted closure and a reason that his wife had senselessly lost her life. After all this time, they had a solid lead, but it was more than Luke had ever bargained for. He couldn't compartmentalize his feelings for Shannon into a little box. He'd crossed a line that should have never been crossed.

SHANNON LAY IN BED missing her baby and feeling twitchy that Luke had stepped outside to find a pay phone to make his call to his superior in Ottawa. What else did she expect but to be treated like a criminal?

Maybe she should have that shower before they really started treating her like a criminal. She started gathering up the photos and guest lists that Luke had left on the bed before he'd run out to make his call, only taking with him the photo of Eldon Winthrop and the guest lists with Winthrop's name on them. Shannon assumed he'd be back to collect the rest.

Idly she sifted through the photos. Would she find a photo of Luke's wife in there if they were pictures taken at functions Mary Calder had attended? Shannon had seen Mary Calder's driver's-license photo of course, but that glimpse had been well over a year ago.

Shannon cast a quick glance at a newspaper clipping from the society column that featured several color photos. A photo at the top of the column of a glamorous-looking couple in their mid-forties captured her attention. Shannon stared at the woman's white fur coat. It looked bitingly familiar with its peculiar black tails hanging from it. As did the woman's blond tumbling hairdo and overdone makeup. But it was the ring on the woman's wedding finger that jolted her memory back into the past. The ring had an unusual butterfly shape. Four large glittering diamonds set in gold, plus the antennae with two diamond chips. Shannon had thought it incredibly tacky when the hand wearing it had pulled Mary Calder's ID from the purse, but now she saw that the stones were all too real and incredibly expensive.

Her heart pounded in her chest as she scanned the caption beneath the photo: "Silver stars sparkled in the sky and on Anya Jennings's stunning silver dress as Mr. and Mrs. Hugh Jennings celebrated their twenty-fifth wedding anniversary with two hundred of their closest friends at a special party at the Hull Casino.''

Shannon read the article detailing the events of the party, Anya's $40,000 dress and the celebrities in attendance, and jumped out of bed. She had to show this to Luke!

But the moment she opened the door to the hall, her path was blocked by a police officer, who looked as if he'd chewed nails for breakfast and didn't give a damn that she needed to see Officer Calder immediately.

She could only imagine what jail would feel like. Guards looking at you as if you were the lowest of life forms. Shannon backed into the room. She'd just page Luke, then. He had to be in the hospital somewhere.

She was trying to accomplish this task on the phone when a brisk knock sounded at the door and her doctor sailed into the room, white coat flapping around his thighs, a stethoscope draping his neck.

He flashed her a smile that was more automatic than sincere. So he knew she was going to be arrested once he released her, too. ''I'm running behind on my rounds today. Would you mind sitting on the bed while I examine you? How are you feeling?'' Shannon reluctantly eased the phone back into the cradle. Her conversation with Luke would have to wait. She had to make arrangements with the doctor for Samantha's care. She just hoped that Luke would return before the police showed up to arrest her.

''THE GUARD TOLD ME I'd find you here. Vaughn says you've got a picture of the suspect? I want it circulating.''

Luke looked up from his game of hide the teddy bear with Samantha as Corporal Donaldson entered the brightly painted hospital room. "The picture's there on the cabinet. So are the guest lists. The mother's certain that's the man who abducted her. Has Vaughn had any luck tracking him down yet?"

"Haven't heard back from him, but I want to get the photo circulating." Donaldson looked at the photo, then peered down into Samantha's crib, a smile warming his face as Samantha lifted up a corner of her blanket and cautiously peeked under it, searched for the stuffed bear. "She's a lucky little girl."

"Very lucky," Luke agreed, whisking the toy out from its hiding spot behind his back and neatly dropping it behind her. "Here's the bear, Sammy." Samantha twisted around, the faint-pink skin on her cheeks and arms a visual reminder of how close she'd come to losing her life.

Samantha pounced on the toy, losing her balance and toppling onto the mattress in the process. "Ba!" She giggled up at him as she chewed on the bear's ear.

Luke chuckled. "That's the way to bring the suspect down." He cupped her head with his hand, marveling on a deeply emotional level how miraculously delicate her tiny body was, hoping she'd be blessed with her mother's strength and courage. The doctor had told him a few minutes ago that he'd release Samantha to her grandmother later in the day. "I've got to go back to work now, Sammy."

"The doctor's released the mother," Donaldson said. "We'll be taking her in."

Luke nodded slowly, knowing there was no longer a way to delay this moment. Every footstep that brought him closer to Shannon's room on the second floor seemed to resonate in his heart. He hoped she'd made good use of her time and phoned a lawyer.

Shannon had showered and changed into the blue shorts and white tank top Alice had brought. The frantic expression that flitted across her face when he and Donaldson entered her hospital room tore at him.

She thrust a newspaper clipping toward him. "This is the woman who sold me your wife's ID. Her name is Anya Jennings. And the man who read the toast at her twenty-fifth wedding-anniversary party is none other than Eldon Winthrop. Do you think there's a connection?"

Chapter Fifteen

Shannon could feel Luke's eyes on her at her arraignment hearing as the court clerk read out the charges against her. Could feel his steadying presence from his seat near the door at the rear of the courtroom. Her knees trembled. There was really only one right thing to do.

"How do you plead?" the judge asked her.

Shannon met the judge's dark questioning gaze. "Guilty, Your Honor."

The Crown prosecutor rose and read the details of her offense, then spoke about what he felt was an appropriate sentence. Shannon had never been so ashamed to hear her actions described in such a public forum. Her attempt to defraud the bank and obtain a loan using her victim's credit history. The pain she'd inflicted on the victim's husband when he'd been notified someone had been using his wife's identity. Her lawyer, however, stressed the mitigating circumstances—that the justice system had failed to protect her from her abusive ex-husband and that she was taking full responsibility for her actions.

Shannon didn't stop holding her breath until the

judge decided to adjourn the proceedings for five weeks so that a Presentence Report could be completed. The prosecutor insisted bail be set as she was a proved flight risk, but her lawyer convinced the judge that since her ex-husband no longer posed a threat to her life, she had no reason to run.

She was free to go until her sentencing hearing.

She thanked her lawyer and hugged her aunt, who was in the courtroom. Then turned to look for Luke. His seat was empty.

He'd already left the courtroom.

SHANNON FRETTED, only paying half a mind to her mother and aunt's questions as they sat on Shannon's porch after Samantha had been cuddled, admired, fussed over and finally put to bed two hours past her normal bedtime. Shannon kept turning her head toward the trees that formed a screen between her property and the rest of the resort. There were lights on in Abner's cottage.

"Shannon," her mother said, stroking her fingers through Shannon's hair, "I have the feeling there's something you're not telling us. I can see it in your face. Out with it now." Shannon had a sudden longing to be a little girl again, her light-brown hair long enough to reach between her shoulder blades, her problems capable of being solved by her mother.

Shannon stared out toward the lake, trying not to be drawn by the lights at Abner's cottage. What was Luke doing now? Still following the investigation? Packing his bags to go back to Ottawa? The thought of his leaving left her feeling terribly unsettled. So much seemed unsaid between them. But what more, really, was there to say?

She'd already apologized for hurting him. She shifted restlessly on the step, slapping at a mosquito that wasn't intimidated by the bug-repelling candles her aunt Jayne had lit and arranged on the railing. Shannon felt as if the battalion of candles was intended to protect her from evil. Corporal Donaldson had told her that arrest warrants had been issued for both Anya Jennings and Eldon Winthrop, but their whereabouts were unknown. Shannon had voiced her suspicions to Corporal Donaldson that someone else—Anya?—had been in the house during her abduction, caring for Samantha. She'd also told the police where Mary's ID cards were hidden in her cottage. She knew they were checking them for Anya's fingerprints, but she didn't know if they'd succeeded.

"Shannon?" her mother prodded, pulling her from her thoughts.

"It's hard to describe, Mom."

"Ah, she has feelings for him, Norah," Aunt Jayne said, her sharp nose bobbing as she nodded knowingly.

"I didn't say that," Shannon objected, wishing her aunt weren't so observant.

Her mother's gaze narrowed on her. "Then what are you saying?"

Shannon shrugged. She couldn't tell her mother or her aunt what had happened between her and Luke. Couldn't ask them if they thought his actions had been real or contrived because he wanted information from her. Maybe the way he'd walked out of the courtroom this afternoon had been answer enough. Maybe she should leave it alone.

LUKE HEARD THE CRICKETS interrupt their song long before he saw the person emerge from the trees. Tension crouched in his stomach like a panther ready to pounce as he sat on the front steps of Abner's cottage, one ear cocked for the phone to ring. Then he saw the moonlight glint off Shannon's hair.

"What are you doing here?" he asked roughly, perhaps too roughly when she came within speaking distance.

She halted in her tracks. Luke noted the indecision in the stiffness of her shoulders. She hugged the paper bag she carried close to her chest. "I'm sorry to intrude."

"You shouldn't be out alone, wandering in the dark. Winthrop is still on the loose. He could be anywhere. The police have extra patrols in the area, but still, Samantha needs you in one piece. You're the only witness to what he's done."

"I was worried about you. I brought you some dinner." She held the bag out to him. "My aunt Jayne makes wonderful stir-fry."

"Thanks, but I'm not very hungry." Telling his family and Mary's mother that they had warrants out for two suspects in Mary's murder and that a woman had pleaded guilty to using Mary's identity had left him without an appetite. Their anger-ridden words questioning how anyone could do such a thing still reverberated in his brain. His mother and mother-in-law were particularly outraged that Shannon wasn't being held in custody until sentencing.

Shannon set the bag on the steps beside him, anyway. "I guess I should have taken the hint when you left the courtroom. I thought you'd be pleased that I pleaded guilty. You won't have to testify against me."

He shot his hand out and caught her wrist. A mistake. A definite mistake. Her skin felt vibrant, feminine and within his power. Luke didn't want to let go. "Is that why you pleaded guilty?"

"No. I pleaded guilty because I am guilty, and the real Shannon Mulligan takes responsibility for her actions."

Luke rose from the step, realizing that the decision he'd been wrestling with had already been made. Resolved in the reaction of his body to the feel of her skin. In what he knew to be true in his heart—even if his feelings might hurt other people that he cared about. "Shannon Mulligan is one hell of a lady." He drew his thumb across her wrist, his gaze drifting to her lips. Slowly he lowered his head, making his intentions clear that he wanted to kiss her. Maybe a future between them was completely impossible, given the situation, but he'd never know unless he kissed her again with all the cards, so to speak, laid out on the table. Anticipation tumbled through him, rich and heady.

"Luke," Shannon whispered, her eyes wide in the dark. "Is it Shannon or Mary you're about to kiss?"

Luke froze, his lips a hairbreadth from hers. "Is that what you think? That I kissed you the other day because you bear a passing resemblance to Mary?"

"It crossed my mind. As did the possibility that you kissed me because you were desperate enough to get the information you needed out of me by any means possible. But I rejected that option. You might have lied to me about who you are, but your actions never lied to me about the kind of man you are. I only wish I'd accepted your advice sooner. Eldon Winthrop and Anya Jennings might be under arrest by now."

He drew a deep shuddering breath and touched his forehead to hers. "Okay. Well, here's an honest answer. Yes, the first time I saw you from a distance I noticed the resemblance in the color of your hair and the way you move. Mary had this inner confidence that showed in every step she took, every word she said. She knew what she wanted and she went after it. And you have that same quality. But from the moment I saw you up close, I've only been aware of the differences. I only see Shannon's hazel eyes and Shannon's beautiful freckles and Shannon's long and lovely legs. It's Shannon's personality that I react to. Shannon's dreams to have her own successful business and raise her daughter that I applaud. And Shannon's strength and courage to do the unthinkable to save herself that I admire. And when I think of touching you, it's the texture and scent of your skin and your hair that I visualize...that I crave. It drove me crazy wanting you, knowing that those feelings could be considered an act of betrayal to my wife. That's why I left the courtroom. I felt terrible for being glad that you were being released until your sentencing hearing. I needed to tell my family and Mary's what had happened in the courtroom. And I knew they'd be upset."

He felt her stiffen.

"I loved her, Shannon. When she died I felt as if someone had not only killed my wife, but also all the dreams we'd shared. And I felt so guilty that I was a cop and whoever had killed her was still roaming the streets. Had you not stolen her identity, the police probably would never have solved her murder. We might not know the specific events that led Winthrop to kill her yet, but I'm confident the police are going to flush him and Anya Jennings out of the woodwork soon."

He caught the fingers of her other hand. "I don't think Mary would hold your crimes against you. Loving her taught me that life is precarious and love a rare and cherished thing. I have feelings for you, Shannon, that I can't deny. And I don't want to deny them any longer. I've spent the last sixteen months feeling disconnected from life and the things I used to enjoy. All I could focus on was the minute-by-minute day-by-day of getting through. I came here thinking I'd check the situation out, report you if you were an imposter, but I never expected to find *myself,* or meet a mother and daughter who made me feel glad to be alive. I never expected to entertain dreams about sharing my life with you and Samantha...but I have."

His words thrilled and frightened Shannon. She jerked her hands from his. "I'm in no position to dream, Luke. My lawyer told me what the potential penalties are. I could go to jail for years. I can't ask you to wait for me."

"You're not asking. I'm offering."

"I'm not accepting. It's too high a price."

"I think I'm getting the better part of the deal. A wife. A daughter."

"I don't think your family or Mary's will be so open-minded."

"They'll change their minds when they get to know you."

"But I don't even know anything about you. All those things that Luke Mathews told me about his family—your brother getting a divorce, nieces, nephews. Was that all lies?"

"I have one brother and one sister, who are both happily married and living in Ottawa. The nieces and nephews are real. My dad is a retired elementary-school principal. My mother still works as a real-estate agent. I worked in construction a few summers while I was in university, and I've been a patrol cop for six years. Before Mary died, I was renovating our house—doing the work myself and enjoying every minute of it. And we were trying to start a family." Shannon didn't want to hear any more. It was easier to refuse his preposterous suggestion when she thought of him only as the cop who'd exposed her secret. Not as a man who enjoyed creating and working with tools as much as she did. And who dreamed of owning his own home and having a family, too.

"No. I can't." The words escaped from her throat. Final.

He exhaled sharply, the breath fanning her face, making her ache to put her arms around him. Draw him nearer until their bodies fit. "Then kiss me good-bye."

"What?"

"I'm not going to argue with you, Shannon. Kiss me goodbye and have a nice life."

Shannon realized he meant it. "Luke, I—"

"Shh. Don't say anything. Just kiss me."

The urgency in his tone pulled at her. She tilted her head back, her nose brushing his cheek, her lips seeking his. She knew the second his lips descended on hers that he'd tricked her. Heat and need fused them together as their tongues sought and found each other. Found comfort and joy and the promise of ecstasy. The taste of him filled her, washed over her senses, made her frantic to have him inside her. Now.

Too many years had passed, years that she'd spent alone, needing, wanting, wondering if there was supposed to be something more than an existence of always being strong. She didn't want to be strong now. She wanted to be weak, to lean, to feel Luke's hands lift her, hold her, join her, make her experience the wonder and the exhilaration of the force of what was happening between them.

She pulled at his T-shirt, needing to feel his flesh beneath her palms. The sleek ridges of muscle and bone. The heat and the male hardness of him. So solid. So Luke.

She could hold on to him forever.

Together they stumbled up the steps, hands reaching out to open the screen door. The slap of it closing behind them. The lights inside suddenly switched off. Clothes lifted, flew, landed like flower petals at their feet. And always, there was the urgency. Her sharp gasp of breath as Luke's hand possessed her breast, the strong fingers molding her flesh, making her knees go weak with the need to have so much more from him. The wet heat of his mouth circling her breast, laving her nipple, brought a moan of deep contentment from her throat.

He went down on his knees before her, kissing each rib, tracing her hips and the curve of her belly with his mouth. Shannon had never felt so feminine, so desired, so cherished. Her body seemed to blossom under his tender ministrations, opening, craving for fulfillment only Luke could give. When he slipped a finger deep inside her, her hips arched forward, showing him how fiercely she wanted this intimacy with him.

"Are you ready for me, sweetheart?"

Shannon whimpered. "Love me, Luke. Just love me."

He smiled up at her, gray-blue eyes gleaming with such triumph that her heart folded in two at the thought that this good man wanted to be hers. All of her adult life she'd been waiting for a moment like this.

"I thought you'd never ask," he growled. Luke stood, lifting her up, her legs wrapped tightly around his waist. He took a few steps in the dark and set her on the edge of a table—or perhaps a counter. Shannon didn't know. Didn't care. She reached for him, guiding him inside her, glorying in the sensation of finally being joined with him, hip to hip, heart to heart.

That first deep thrust completed her in a way she'd never imagined. She met it with everything she had in her, rode the wave of pleasure and climbed high again with the next one. Harder, faster.

Luke held on to Shannon for dear life, thrusting his

hopes and dreams into her body, whispering in her ear the words that filled his heart, his soul soaring at the words she whispered back. He'd never expected to experience love again. To have the dreams that had been ripped from him restored through the love of another woman. Shannon felt so right with him. So very very right. Sweet heaven, she was coming! Luke could feel her tremors wrap around him with velvet tension. Felt his own tightly reined control slipping dizzily away…until the faint creak of a floorboard pierced his senses and brought him reeling back to his surroundings.

He moved instinctively, pulling Shannon with him off the counter to the floor as a gunshot rang out. A second shot split the wood in the cabinet door above his head.

Someone was on the porch with a gun!

FEAR SPILLED through Luke as his thoughts raced toward controlling the situation and surviving. Wordlessly he pushed Shannon behind the kitchen counter for cover. Like Shannon's cottage, the phone was an older wall-mounted model. If they could reach it, help wouldn't be far off.

The slap of the screen door gave the shooter's location away. Another shot rang out, striking the window above the sink. Luke quickly opened a bottom cupboard, feeling inside for the pots and pans he knew to be there. He handed one to Shannon, then lifted a saucepan and hurled it over the counter toward the door. At the same time, he made a grab for the phone. Shannon threw her pan across the room to cover him.

Another shot rang out and the phone slipped from his fingers—the dial tone sounding like a warning buzzer—as his body jerked from the impact of a bullet entering his chest.

The phone hit the floor seconds before Luke did.

He felt Shannon's hands on him.

"Luke!"

"Shh! Dial 911," he told her, instinctively pushing her up close to the cabinet. The counter was too wide for their assailant to reach over and shoot them. He'd have to come into the U-shaped kitchen. Luke reached into the cupboard for another pot. His chest felt strangely numb. They only had an advantage as long as the lights were out. His fingers closed around a heavy cast-iron frying pan. He slid along the floor toward the opening between the counters.

He could hear the emergency dispatcher's voice asking questions. Shannon wasn't responding, thank God. Still, if Luke could hear the dispatcher's voice, so could their assailant.

Then everything happened fast. Luke sensed the assailant's approach and backhanded him with the heavy frying pan, giving it all he had. Their assailant cried out and the gun went off. Luke let out a muffled cry of his own as excruciating pain shattered his lower right leg. He took another backhanded swing at the perp, feeling a solid connection. Then to his horror he heard Shannon scrambling onto the countertop. She launched herself onto their assailant, catching him off guard and sending them both crashing to the floor. Luke heard the unmistakable clatter of the gun hitting the wooden floor. Shannon was screaming.

Steely shards of fear pierced Luke's heart. He had to get the gun!

He pulled himself along the floor, trying to ignore the clamoring of pain in his leg, his fingers moving over the floor in a desperate attempt to locate the gun.

His fingers grazed something. *There!*

His fingers were just curling around the butt of the gun and finding home on the trigger when he heard the screen door open.

Luke knew it wasn't a cop. A cop would identify himself. The lights came on.

Luke blinked. He saw a woman, unarmed, at the door, dressed in a skin-tight black outfit, terror etched on her face. Anya Jennings. Then he saw Winthrop straddling Shannon, his fingers around her neck.

Time seemed to slow to a standstill. Luke squeezed off two shots in rapid succession. One bullet hit Winthrop between the shoulder blades, the second hit him in the back of the head. He slumped forward over Shannon.

Luke turned the gun on Anya as she rushed forward with a sharp wail. "No!"

"Police. Freeze or I'll shoot," Luke ordered her, trying to keep from drifting into the gray haze that was settling over his brain.

Anya paused briefly, then came at him, screaming, nails raised like claws, the makeup piled on her face smudging into a black blur before Luke's eyes. "We waited so long—"

Luke didn't give her a chance to finish her sentence or get any closer. He squeezed the trigger twice. She could join Winthrop in an early grave. Surprise registered on Anya's face as the bullets pumped into her body. She crumpled to the floor.

"Shannon, are you injured?" he asked, keeping his eyes and the gun trained on Anya. She wasn't moving.

"I'm all right. I just can't get him off me!"

Relief washed through Luke. Struggling to stay conscious, he called out the situation to the dispatcher on the phone. Shannon succeeded in extricating herself from beneath Winthrop's body just as the police surrounded the cottage and ordered them out. Luke instructed Shannon, who had grabbed a roll of paper towels off the counter and was bunching it into compresses to put on his chest and leg, to pull on her clothes and go out, taking his badge with her. "Hurry," he urged her when she started to protest. He could feel what little strength was within him draining away. "Tell them Winthrop and Anya Jennings are probably dead and that I'm injured and where we are in the room. I've got enough bullets in me—I don't want to get blown away by a cop trying to distinguish the good guys from the bad guys."

Fear that he might not survive his wounds prompted him to add as she crossed the threshold, "By the way, that was one hell of a goodbye."

The look she sent him over her shoulder cut to his heart. Then she was gone.

Luke laid down the gun and passed out.

Chapter Sixteen

Shannon hadn't expected Luke to be in the courtroom for her sentencing hearing. Five weeks had passed since that horrible night when Eldon Winthrop had burst into Luke's cottage and shot at them. Shannon hadn't seen Luke since he'd been loaded into an ambulance.

Corporal Donaldson had told her that Luke had been taken to the Penticton hospital, then airlifted to a hospital in Calgary for treatment. When Shannon had called the Calgary hospital and asked to be connected to Luke's room, a woman had answered the phone and offered to take a message, because Luke was resting.

But Shannon heard the cold fury in the woman's voice the instant Shannon stated her name. "I'm Luke's mother. He's alive, no thanks to you. He made it through surgery, though the doctors are concerned about a possible spinal-cord injury from the bullet that entered his chest. We need to wait for the swelling to subside. The doctors also told us he'll need some rehabilitation for his leg—the bone was broken. Please don't call back. You've already done more than enough to hurt my son, maybe even ruined his career. I can't say it plainer than that.''

Shannon had hung up the phone, numb with remorse. Two sleepless days and nights later, her aunt managed to get an update on Luke's condition. The swelling had gone down, and Luke was expected to make a full recovery. Shannon had sent him a ''get well'' card with one word written on it: Goodbye.

She had no idea whether or not he'd received it. She hadn't heard from him. She supposed he had no reason to contact her. Though Luke had shot and killed Eldon Winthrop, Anya Jennings had survived her injuries and confessed to the police, explaining that she and Eldon Winthrop had been having an affair for years behind her husband's back. Eldon had let rumors abound that he was gay to keep his partner from becoming suspicious. But when his partner mentioned that he suspected his wife was involved with another man, Eldon feared Jennings would soon stumble on the truth—or had already—especially when his partner phoned him the day of the St. Patrick's party and insisted they meet privately that night, as he had an urgent matter to discuss. Killing Jennings seemed the most expedient means of keeping the commercial-real-estate business he'd built with Jennings intact and having Anya for his own. But Anya had told the police that Eldon Winthrop had encountered Mary on the back stairs of the country club. She'd been on her way upstairs to meet with a client in a private lounge. Winthrop was descending the stairs, holding a glass that contained the remnants of the drink he'd given his partner. He'd dissolved enough sleeping pills in the drink to knock Jennings unconscious, which had enabled him to inject a lethal dose of potassium chloride into his partner's bloodstream.

Ever the public-relations rep, Mary had stopped him and introduced herself. Eldon and Anya had worked so hard to establish alibis that they couldn't take the chance she'd remember seeing him at the party. So he went back upstairs to the lounge and used Jennings's cell phone to call Anya. He told her to meet him at his car. They waited for Mary to leave and followed her. Winthrop had attacked her when she stopped at a light at a dark intersection.

Eldon had given Mary's purse to Anya with instructions to dispose of it in a seedy part of town on her way home where it would get picked up by some low-life, thus leading the police in an erroneous direction. Only, Shannon had come upon Anya on the street and mistaken her for a prostitute.

Taken aback by Shannon's request for stolen ID, Anya had gathered her wits and sold her Mary's ID for a nominal sum. They'd committed a perfect crime, had nearly gotten away with it, except that Eldon Winthrop had realized the police were suspicious and keeping tabs on him, which made him wonder if Mary Calder might somehow have survived her attack, but not remember everything that had happened. Eldon had grown worried when Luke had suddenly left town. He'd used his considerable influence to track Luke down. Constable Donaldson seemed certain from interrogating Anya that until the moment he'd died, Eldon Winthrop was convinced that Shannon was the real Mary Calder. Anya had never recognized Shannon as the woman she'd sold the stolen ID to. But she had revealed to the police the location of the rental cottage where she and Eldon had laid low after the fire. When they realized from media reports that a woman and infant had survived, they knew Mary could identify Eldon. They risked night watches on Shady Pines, waiting for an opportunity to get Mary and Luke alone. That opportunity arrived when Shannon had walked over to Abner's cottage.

Shannon sighed, her heart filling with a mixture of emotions as her gaze rested on Luke. He looked thinner, but still so handsome in khaki pants and a navy-blue golf shirt. Her heart squeezed in instant response to his presence.

He was flanked by a cluster of people. On his right was an attractive woman in her late fifties, her lips tightly compressed. That surely was his mother. The older gentleman, whose broad shoulders and body build resembled Luke's, must be his father. Oh, God, had they all come to see she was punished? Shannon guessed the other people were Luke's brother and sister and their spouses.

She could feel their eyes on her in the gallery, judging her, and she turned away, her heart heavy at the grief she'd caused them.

Her palms were damp with sweat when the court clerk called her name. Shannon felt her legs bend like plastic straws as she went to stand by her lawyer at the defense table. It was going to be very bad, she thought as the judge began recounting the seriousness of her offense. "A jail sentence of eighteen months would not be unreasonable,'' the judge stated, then paused.

Shannon tried to hold fast to her courage. Eighteen months! Samantha would be almost three by the time she was released. "However," the judge continued, "there is no doubt in my mind that you were abused by your former husband. You made numerous efforts to seek protection from him via the courts, and the justice system clearly let you down. You have been through a difficult time, and you have shown remorse for your actions. You have no previous convictions, and I've noted that you cooperated fully with the authorities when informed that the woman whose identity you had stolen had been murdered, and that information led to an arrest. After weighing all the factors, this court grants you a conditional discharge. You are sentenced to seek counseling for the trauma you've experienced and to perform 240 hours of community service, preferably at a shelter for battered women."

Shannon stared up at the judge, shock welling through her. A conditional discharge meant she wouldn't have a criminal record! "Does the sentence have to be carried out in British Columbia?" she asked meekly. "I would like to return to my family in Halifax."

The judge smiled at her. "No. Your probation officer can arrange a Transfer of Jurisdiction for me to sign."

"Thank you, Your Honor."

Shannon's lawyer took her by the arm and escorted her out into the hallway. She was still trying to absorb the judge's decision when her mother and aunt surrounded her, wrapping her in exuberant hugs. "You and Samantha can come live with Jayne and me," Norah said, her cheeks wet with tears. "There's plenty of room."

"And plenty of free baby-sitting," Aunt Jayne added, laughing.

Shannon's mind whirled. Being with her mother and aunt again would be wonderful, but—

A husky male voice cut through the laughter and went straight to Shannon's heart. "Excuse me, may I have a private word with Shannon?"

Luke. Heat flared in her cheeks as her mother and aunt excused themselves and promised to wait in the car. Shannon didn't know what to say to Luke after all this time, after the judge's sentence. Were he and his family disappointed by the judge's decision? Satisfied? Her gaze centered on Luke's chest and slid downward, as if reassuring herself that he was all in one piece. His slacks had been cut to accommodate the cast on his right leg. Finally her eyes flickered up to meet the unwavering gray-blue gaze of the man she'd made love to so fervently that the thought of those precious minutes made her pulse race. Farther down the hall she could see his family gathered, overtly watching them. "How are you?"

"Mending. Doing light duty. I should be back in a patrol car in a few weeks."

"I'm so glad." Shannon couldn't help herself. She touched his arm, knowing that his family was watching. The heat of his skin seared her fingertips as if warning her that even such a small touch between them was forbidden. She reluctantly drew her hand away. "I was so scared. You saved me—not just physically, but emotionally—and I'll always be grateful to you for that."

"You saved me, too." She felt his gaze skim over her face, felt her stomach tumble at the way his eyes lingered on her mouth. "I like the brown hair. It suits you."

Shannon self-consciously touched her hair. "It's the real me."

"How's Samantha?"

"Beautiful! Growing." Shannon bit her tongue to keep from telling him how Samantha had noticed his absence, how she seemed to be looking for Luke to play with. "I had a visit from Dylan and Donna White. Something you said to Dylan must have had some effect. He apologized for spying on me and making crank phone calls. He swore he didn't have anything to do with the break-in at Glorie's or slitting my tire or throwing the rocks. I believe him. I think Rob was trying to scare me."

"Rob didn't stand a chance." Luke tilted his head to one side, sensing the tension beneath her clipped sentences. The rational part of his mind told him to respect the goodbye card she'd sent him, but his heart had its own agenda. "Congratulations on the sentence. So what are you going to do with your life now?"

"My mother has dropped broad hints that she'd like me to move back home to Halifax. I guess I'll start another crafts business there. How about you?"

Luke figured he had nothing to lose by putting his

feelings on the line. "I was thinking about getting married and having a family—with you."

Shannon felt the blood drain from her face. Luke would be the kind of husband most women only dream about marrying. But it couldn't be her dream. Not if it meant hurting him and his family. "Luke, I am so honored that you feel that way for me after everything I've done. But look at your family…at the expressions on their faces. They would never accept me. And what about your friends and your job? How would they feel about you getting involved with a criminal?"

Luke didn't turn around to look. His gaze remained locked with hers. "You're not a criminal. Any friend or family member who professes to care about me would want me to be happy and would give you a fair chance. And the idea of spending my life with you and Samantha makes me very happy. I love you whether you want me to or not. Whether it's easy or not. The question is whether or not you feel the same way about me."

Tears burned in Shannon's eyes as she stayed silent, convinced she was doing what was best for him even as she saw the desire in his eyes cool to disappointment and the grim line of acceptance firm in his jaw at her lack of a response. He turned away, his shoulders bearing the stamp of resigned loneliness that she'd often glimpsed in her own shoulders. Each slow hobbled step took him farther from her heart, from her life.

Her heart cried foul. How could she let him go, this man who'd treated her with such loving respect? She'd had the courage to walk away from her marriage to

Rob and the courage to plead guilty to the crime she'd committed; surely she had the courage to tell Luke how much she loved him and would deal with whatever gossip or problems might come their way?

"Luke, wait!" She ran after him, her heart pounding. "I just don't want you to be ashamed of me. Ever. Not when you're so...good."

Luke stopped, awkwardly swinging around on his cast, hope banked in his eyes. "Ashamed of what? That you're a survivor? That you built your own business? Proud is more like it."

"Really? What about the community service?"

"Here's a news flash for you. I'd still want to marry you even if you'd been given a jail term. I think the judge realized you could be great helping out at a women's shelter. Where's the shame in helping women escape an abusive situation? You know better than anyone how much support a woman needs."

Support. Shannon lifted her chin, her throat tightening with emotion. Luke had offered her love and support and trust. Treasured gifts that she could repay him in kind for the rest of her life if she had the courage to accept them. She laid her hand on his chest, felt the steady thrum of his heart, felt desire for him warm her to her toes. "I love you, Luke. Will you do me the honor of becoming my husband and Samantha's father?"

Luke's breath hitched. "Did I just hear you ask me to marry you?"

She smiled up at him. "Very gutsy of me, I know. But I met this man who told me I should have the courage to ask for what I want. And I want you,

Luke.'' She lowered her voice to a whisper. ''If your family weren't standing so near, I'd tell you exactly how much I want you.''

Luke's eyes glowed with a heat that stirred joy in Shannon's heart. His mouth slid into an easy grin. ''Shannon Calder. I like the sound of that. But what do you say we make it legal this time? Samantha, too.''

''Yes, very legal,'' Shannon agreed as Luke's lips hungrily claimed hers in a kiss that took her to heaven.

The sound of applause brought her back to earth. Luke's family was clapping. Shannon and Luke broke apart, laughing. Luke's mother joined them, her hand outstretched, and she was smiling. ''Luke's told us so much about you, Shannon, in the last few weeks. I hope you can forgive me for being an overprotective mother on the phone. Welcome to the family.''

Shannon couldn't see for the tears blurring her eyes as Luke's family surrounded them, joking and making introductions. Being a real Calder would be a joy.

HARLEQUIN®
INTRIGUE®

43
Light St.

has been *the* address for outstanding
romantic suspense for more than a decade!
Now REBECCA YORK* blasts the hinges
off the front door with a new trilogy—
MINE TO KEEP.

Look for these great stories on the corner of
heart-stopping romance and breathtaking suspense!

THE MAN FROM TEXAS
August 2001

NEVER ALONE
October 2001

LASSITER'S LAW
December 2001

COME ON OVER...
WE'LL KEEP THE LIGHTS ON.

Available at your favorite retail outlet.

*Ruth Glick writing as Rebecca York

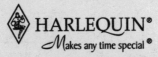

COMING SOON...

AN EXCITING
OPPORTUNITY TO SAVE
ON THE PURCHASE OF
HARLEQUIN AND
SILHOUETTE BOOKS!

*DETAILS TO FOLLOW
IN OCTOBER 2001!*

YOU WON'T WANT TO MISS IT!

PHQ401

HARLEQUIN®
Makes any time special®

Silhouette®
Where love comes alive™

Harlequin truly does make any time special. . . . This year we are celebrating weddings in style!

A Walk Down the Aisle

WEDDING CELEBRATION

To help us celebrate, we want you to tell us how wearing the Harlequin wedding gown will make your wedding day special. As the grand prize, Harlequin will offer one lucky bride the chance to **"Walk Down the Aisle" in the Harlequin wedding gown!**

There's more...

For her honeymoon, she and her groom will spend five nights at the **Hyatt Regency Maui.** As part of this five-night honeymoon at the hotel renowned for its romantic attractions, the couple will enjoy a candlelit dinner for two in Swan Court, a sunset sail on the hotel's catamaran, and duet spa treatments.

A HYATT RESORT AND SPA

Maui • Molokai • Lanai

To enter, please write, in, 250 words or less, how wearing the Harlequin wedding gown will make your wedding day special. The entry will be judged based on its emotionally compelling nature, its originality and creativity, and its sincerity. This contest is open to Canadian and U.S. residents only and to those who are 18 years of age and older. There is no purchase necessary to enter. Void where prohibited. See further contest rules attached. Please send your entry to:

Walk Down the Aisle Contest

In Canada	In U.S.A.
P.O. Box 637	P.O. Box 9076
Fort Erie, Ontario	3010 Walden Ave.
L2A 5X3	Buffalo, NY 14269-9076

You can also enter by visiting www.eHarlequin.com
Win the Harlequin wedding gown and the vacation of a lifetime!
The deadline for entries is October 1, 2001.

HARLEQUIN®
Makes any time special ®

PHWDACONT1

1. To enter, follow directions published in the offer to which you are responding. Contest begins April 2, 2001, and ends on October 1, 2001. Method of entry may vary. Mailed entries must be postmarked by October 1, 2001, and received by October 8, 2001.

2. Contest entry may be, at times, presented via the Internet, but will be restricted solely to residents of certain georgraphic areas that are disclosed on the Web site. To enter via the Internet, if permissible, access the Harlequin Web site (www.eHarlequin.com) and follow the directions displayed online. Online entries must be received by 11:59 p.m. E.S.T. on October 1, 2001.

   In lieu of submitting an entry online, enter by mail by hand-printing (or typing) on an 8½" x 11" plain piece of paper, your name, address (including zip code), Contest number/name and in 250 words or fewer, why winning a Harlequin wedding dress would make your wedding day special. Mail via first-class mail to: Harlequin Walk Down the Aisle Contest 1197, (in the U.S.) P.O. Box 9076, 3010 Walden Avenue, Buffalo, NY 14269-9076, (in Canada) P.O. Box 637, Fort Erie, Ontario L2A 5X3, Canada.

   Limit one entry per person, household address and e-mail address. Online and/or mailed entries received from persons residing in geographic areas in which Internet entry is not permissible will be disqualified.

3. Contests will be judged by a panel of members of the Harlequin editorial, marketing and public relations staff based on the following criteria:

   - Originality and Creativity—50%
   - Emotionally Compelling—25%
   - Sincerity—25%

   In the event of a tie, duplicate prizes will be awarded. Decisions of the judges are final.

4. All entries become the property of Torstar Corp. and will not be returned. No responsibility is assumed for lost, late, illegible, incomplete, inaccurate, nondelivered or misdirected mail or misdirected e-mail, for technical, hardware or software failures of any kind, lost or unavailable network connections, or failed, incomplete, garbled or delayed computer transmission or any human error which may occur in the receipt or processing of the entries in this Contest.

5. Contest open only to residents of the U.S. (except Puerto Rico) and Canada, who are 18 years of age or older, and is void wherever prohibited by law; all applicable laws and regulations apply. Any litigation within the Province of Quebec respecting the conduct or organization of a publicity contest may be submitted to the Régie des alcools, des courses et des jeux for a ruling. Any litigation respecting the awarding of a prize may be submitted to the Régie des alcools, des courses et des jeux only for the purpose of helping the parties reach a settlement. Employees and immediate family members of Torstar Corp. and D. L. Blair, Inc., their affiliates, subsidiaries and all other agencies, entities and persons connected with the use, marketing or conduct of this Contest are not eligible to enter. Taxes on prizes are the sole responsibility of winners. Acceptance of any prize offered constitutes permission to use winner's name, photograph or other likeness for the purposes of advertising, trade and promotion on behalf of Torstar Corp., its affiliates and subsidiaries without further compensation to the winner, unless prohibited by law.

6. Winners will be determined no later than November 15, 2001, and will be notified by mail. Winners will be required to sign and return an Affidavit of Eligibility form within 15 days after winner notification. Noncompliance within that time period may result in disqualification and an alternative winner may be selected. Winners of trip must execute a Release of Liability prior to ticketing and must possess required travel documents (e.g. passport, photo ID) where applicable. Trip must be completed by November 2002. No substitution of prize permitted by winner. Torstar Corp. and D. L. Blair, Inc., their parents, affiliates, and subsidiaries are not responsible for errors in printing or electronic presentation of Contest, entries and/or game pieces. In the event of printing or other errors which may result in unintended prize values or duplication of prizes, all affected game pieces or entries shall be null and void. If for any reason the Internet portion of the Contest is not capable of running as planned, including infection by computer virus, bugs, tampering, unauthorized intervention, fraud, technical failures, or any other causes beyond the control of Torstar Corp. which corrupt or affect the administration, secrecy, fairness, integrity or proper conduct of the Contest, Torstar Corp. reserves the right, at its sole discretion, to disqualify any individual who tampers with the entry process and to cancel, terminate, modify or suspend the Contest or the Internet portion thereof. In the event of a dispute regarding an online entry, the entry will be deemed submitted by the authorized holder of the e-mail account submitted at the time of entry. Authorized account holder is defined as the natural person who is assigned to an e-mail address by an Internet access provider, online service provider or other organization that is responsible for arranging e-mail address for the domain associated with the submitted e-mail address. **Purchase or acceptance of a product offer does not improve your chances of winning.**

7. Prizes: (1) Grand Prize—A Harlequin wedding dress (approximate retail value: $3,500) and a 5-night/6-day honeymoon trip to Maui, HI, including round-trip air transportation provided by Maui Visitors Bureau from Los Angeles International Airport (winner is responsible for transportation to and from Los Angeles International Airport) and a Harlequin Romance Package, including hotel accomodations (double occupancy) at the Hyatt Regency Maui Resort and Spa, dinner for (2) two at Swan Court, a sunset sail on Kiele V and a spa treatment for the winner (approximate retail value: $4,000); (5) five runner-up prizes of a $1000 gift certificate to selected retail outlets to be determined by Sponsor (retail value $1000 ea.). Prizes consist of only those items listed as part of the prize. Limit one prize per person. All prizes are valued in U.S. currency.

8. For a list of winners (available after December 17, 2001) send a self-addressed, stamped envelope to: Harlequin Walk Down the Aisle Contest 1197 Winners, P.O. Box 4200 Blair, NE 68009-4200 or you may access the www.eHarlequin.com Web site through January 15, 2002.

Contest sponsored by Torstar Corp., P.O. Box 9042, Buffalo, NY 14269-9042, U.S.A.

PHWDACONT2

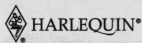

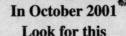

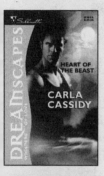
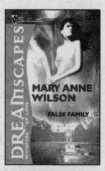

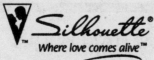